SUMMER PEOPLE

SUMMER PEOPLE

AARON STANDER

Publisher's Cataloging in Publication Data
Stander, Aaron.
Summer People / Aaron Stander. – Interlochen, Mich.: Writers & Editors, 2009.

ISBN: 978-0-9785732-1-8
1. Murder–Michigan–Fiction. 2. Murder–Investigation–Fiction.

Printed and bound in the United States of America

FOR BEACHWALKER

1

~~~~~~

*F*rom a dune near the shore, a telescopic sight cut through the heavy rain and fog. The six figures on the porch were clearly visible—three women to the right and three men to the left. Two clusters, six people at the opposite poles of the long, brightly lit porch.

The cross hairs wheeled along the porch from left to right, stopping at each figure, pausing for a long moment, and then moving on. The scope traveled back across the porch; the cross hairs centered on a woman standing at the far end of the porch. The woman turned and went into the cottage. The sight stopped at the two women seated at a table. They were older than the first, middle-aged. They pulled closer to one another as they talked, moving apart when the third woman rejoined them.

The telescopic sight moved back along the porch to the left, centering on the man with the thinning, blond hair—moving with him, waiting until he leaned forward away from a window pillar, waiting for him to turn sideways, waiting until the profile of his head and neck could be perfectly aligned in the cross hairs.

Randy Holden mixed drinks for his two friends, Robert Austin and Larry James. His wife made coffee for their wives.

"How did you get by the SEC when guys like Ivan Boesky got nailed to the wall?" Robert asked as Randy handed him a gin and tonic.

"Boesky lacked subtlety. He always wanted to make it and show it. He came from nothing. His old man owned a greasy spoon in Detroit before the tribe moved to West Bloomfield. As soon he started making the bucks, he flaunted it. It's sort of a Jewish thing, isn't it?"

"Now Randy," interrupted Larry in a mocking tone, "Aren't religious and ethnic slurs, particularly ones directed against a Cranbrook graduate, in bad taste, especially for old money like you? You must take pity on those not fortunate enough to be born Episcopalian, rich, and with impeccable taste."

Just as Randy started to answer, a long flash of lightning raced across the horizon, vertical bolts crashing into the lake. The lights flickered and went out as the thunder rocked the old cottage. A few seconds later the lights came on again.

"See," said Larry with a broad smile, "even the gods don't condone that kind of bigotry anymore."

"Sarcastic bastard," retorted Randy. "Besides, Ivan never graduated from Cranbrook. He went back to a public school, probably graduated from Mumford or Central. That's where they all went. Anyway, I'll be the Episcopalian Ivan, and I'll have the good sense not to end up in a federal country club. What kind of Scotch do you want?" he asked Larry. "I have Cutty and Black and White."

Larry raised an eyebrow, "I thought you'd stock something a bit more exotic. You always insist on a single malt when you're at my place."

"What can I say? These are the high-end Scotches at the liquor store down the road. We're in the provinces, remember. What are you going to have?" he asked again.

"I'll have the Black and White; it's probably the least likely of the two to burn a hole in my esophagus."

"Good choice, I'll have the same," said Randy. "Soda, water, or neat?"

"Better make it a lot of soda."

Randy turned his back to the other two men as they continued to banter. He pulled two glasses from the shelf, dropped three ice cubes in each, and half-filled the first glass with Scotch from a bottle on the bar. He pulled a second bottle from an obscure corner of the cabinet, taking care to position his body so his guests couldn't see what he was doing, and half-filled the second glass. Turning the label to the back, he hid the bottle from view again. He topped the first glass with soda, placed a paper napkin—a napkin with a silk-screened fern—around the bottom of the glass and served it to Larry. Then he added a splash of soda to his drink and rejoined the conversation.

As he lifted the glass to sip, the window to his right exploded. For an instant he had a slightly sick look; then he collapsed backwards, head loose, body limp. The heavy, amber whiskey tumbler fell. Its bottom edge slammed into the thick, grass-mat flooring, bounced once, turned a perfect 360 as its contents emptied, rolled on its side, and finally came to rest against a lifeless hand.

2

Even in the heavy rain and fog, the flashing lights from a patrol car made the cottage easy to find. Sheriff Ray Elkins was met at the back door by one of his deputies, Jake Howe. As Jake led him through the cottage, Ray noted the layout was like most of the summer homes from the twenties and thirties. The back door opened into the kitchen, the front door led to a screened porch that faced the lake. Between the kitchen and the front porch was a large living room. Usually the bedrooms were on the second floor.

Jake led Ray into the living room. Three couches, forming a "U", were grouped in front of a massive, split-stone fireplace. Two middle-aged couples sat close together on two of the couches. At the far corner of the third couch was a young woman wrapped in an afghan, her feet pulled up, her hands covering her face. Brett Carty, the department's newest deputy, stood behind her looking ill at ease.

"This is Sheriff Elkins," the deputy announced. The men stood. The one nearest Ray extended his hand.

"I'm Doctor James and this is my wife Jean." The woman on the couch next to him gave a weary nod. James gestured toward the couple on the other couch, "Robert Austin, Judy, his wife."

Ray shook hands with the second man; his wife held a fixed gaze on the floor in front of her.

Dr. James gestured to the third woman, "That is Mrs. Holden." The young woman opened her eyes, but didn't move.

"Sheriff, we're all exhausted. Can we get this over with so we can go home?" James asked.

"I'll try to move things along as quickly as possible, sir. But there are certain procedures we have to follow, and they take time." He turned to Jake who led him onto the front porch.

"This is just how I found the victim."

"Did you check outside?"

"After Brett got here I checked the beach and looked around for a vehicle, didn't see nothing. Imagine the shooter was long gone by that time. There's a bunch a two-tracks running to the other cottages, lots of ways to get out of here.

"We'll go over the area in the morning. Given the heavy rain, I don't think we have to worry about losing much."

Ray knelt next to the body; he looked from one side of the victim's neck to the other. "Nicely done."

"How's that?" asked Jake.

"A good shot, accurate, and effective. Looks like the shooter really knew what he was about. I'll question the others; what do you know about them?"

"Not much," said Jake as he pulled a small notebook from his pocket. "The victim is Randy Holden, forty-eight, summer resident, home's in Chicago. The younger woman is the wife of the victim. The other two couples are from around Detroit; they have places up here—Suttons Bay and Old Mission."

Ray returned to the living room and announced to the group that he would be questioning them briefly, one at a time, in the kitchen. He asked Doctor James to follow him, offered him a seat at the kitchen table, and took the chair on the opposite side.

"To the best of your memory, tell me exactly what happened."

"It was close to midnight when we got back here. My wife wanted to go home after the play, but Randy insisted we come out for a nightcap. Randy mixed drinks. He had just handed us our drinks and finished getting his own when the window near him sort of exploded. I looked at the window and then back at him as he fell."

"Then what happened?" asked Ray.

"I started to search for a pulse, but after I saw the wound, I knew that he was dead. By the time I looked up, everyone was around me. I think I said that Randy was dead. For a few seconds we were all sort of frozen. Then Bob's wife became hysterical and started yelling we were all going to get killed. We hurried into the cottage, locked the doors, dialed 911, turned off the lights, and waited for the police."

"How much time passed before the first officer arrived?"

"It probably was only ten or fifteen minutes, but it seemed like hours. Bob's wife was almost out of control. I tried to talk her down."

"And the victim's wife?"

"She was quite calm. I don't think that it sank in right away. Then she just sobbed; my wife tried to comfort her."

Ray nodded. "There are three cars parked here; did you meet here and go as a group?"

"No, we met for dinner and the theater. Then we came out here in our own cars. Actually, we'd been together most of the day."

"How's that?"

"We met, the three of us—Randy, Bob and I—for lunch and golf." He paused.

"Where?"

"At the Resort. We had lunch and then played the Bear. After, the women joined us, everyone came to our place for cocktails. We had dinner at Bowers Inn and went on to the theater."

"And then you came back here. About what time was that?"

"Must have been around 11:30 or 11:45 when we finally got here. With the rain and fog it was slow going. As we were coming up the drive I promised my wife that we would only have a quick drink and go home. She was angry we'd come out here for a nightcap."

"Did you notice other vehicles or any people in the vicinity?"

"I didn't see anything. As I said, it was pouring. I followed Randy out. Bob followed me—sort of a caravan."

"What happened after you arrived?"

"We waited in our cars until Randy had the door open and the lights on, then we ran for the house. We went out on the front porch. Randy started mixing drinks. The girls didn't want any alcohol, so his wife was making coffee."

"Were you all on the porch at the time of the shooting?"

"Yes, Bob and I were almost next to him. The girls were sitting at the table at the other end."

"Did you hear a shot?"

"No, just the window shattering."

"Did you hear any additional shots?"

"No."

"And after the victim was shot, did you see anything, car lights, anything like that?"

"Nothing at all, but my attention was first with Randy and then looking after the women."

"I can appreciate that," said Ray. "I'm just trying to get as complete a picture of the events as possible, so anything that you can remember might be helpful. Can you tell me about the victim? How long have you known him?"

"Years. I met Randy in high school."

"Where was that?"

"Cranbrook, that's in Bloomfield Hills."

Ray nodded without commenting.

"And then we were in the same fraternity at Michigan."

"So you were a close friend of the victim?"

"I wouldn't say close. Randy had a million friends, but I doubt if any of them were close. In recent years I usually saw him only once or twice a year, always up here. We'd get together for golf. Bob was also in the frat, he occasionally joined us."

"Can you tell me anything more about the victim? Do you know why anyone might want to kill him?"

"I've known him for a long time, but our friendship has always been of a casual nature, and after he moved to Chicago, that's about ten years ago, we didn't really see much of each other. But I can tell you this..." He paused and looked at Ray for a long moment. "Let's see, how do I want to say this? Randy was full of himself. He seemed to enjoy giving people the impression that he was a bit out-of-bounds; he liked to say he was 'living on the edge.' It was sort of charming. But I'm sure a steady diet of it would have been rather tedious. I know he was in trouble some years back, and after, he moved on to Chicago. I never knew exactly what the problem was, but some kind of ethics issue got him in trouble with the state bar. As I said, a charming guy, but not someone you'd trust with your retirement."

"Before today, when was the last time you saw him?"

"Probably last August."

"Who arranged this get-together?"

"He did. He called me at the office a couple of weeks ago and asked when I was coming up and if we could get together. He told me he had remarried, and he wanted me to meet his bride." He paused.

"I noticed you smiled when you said, 'meet his bride,'" Ray said.

"As long as I've known Randy, he's always been introducing me to his new woman, bride, whatever."

"He was married before?"

"At least three or four times, and in between he was never without a woman. He seemed to want to show them off like some expensive new toy. I don't think I ever saw any of them more than two or three times."

"Did Mr. Holden say anything yesterday that would suggest that he was in any trouble, or did he appear worried about anything?"

"Nothing at all. Randy was bright, but not deep. I never saw him worry about anything. He told us about how well he was doing, how much we would like his new bride—I guess that's why I liked seeing him occasionally."

"What do you mean?"

"It was like being a college boy again. Sitting around, shooting the bull. It was all so removed from my day-to-day worries.

"Do you know what business he was in?"

"He was a lawyer by training, but after he moved to Chicago I think he mostly worked in investments. He said he was making millions in futures."

"While you were with him yesterday, did anyone approach him or did he have any phone calls?"

"Not to my memory."

"Did he make any phone calls?"

"After we finished playing, he called his wife briefly. I think that's the only call he made."

"So you don't remember anything that might suggest that he was in some sort of trouble?"

"No, nothing. Just the same old Randy. He was full of himself and quite pleased with his new wife. He seemed to bring her into our conversations all afternoon, as if to tell us he had found the fountain of youth. He always needed to brag. Actually Tawny—that's a hell of a name, isn't it—turned out to be quite nice. I don't understand how she hooked up with him. Sorry, Sheriff, I don't know anything else. Getting together with Randy was just a summer thing. I really don't know a hell of a lot about him."

Ray next questioned Robert Austin. He seemed to know even less than the doctor. Their wives added nothing of substance, but both women gave Ray the impression that they disliked Randy. Then he talked with the widow briefly. She was obviously in shock. He decided to put off further questioning until the next day. Dr.

James and his wife offered to take Tawny Holden to their home for the night.

Ray asked Ben to get all the names, addresses, and phone numbers before they left. When he went back out to the front porch, Ray could see that the coroner, Ted Lynch, was kneeling beside the body on the porch. Ray knelt at his side.

"Dead as hell, Sheriff," said Ted.

Ray had always been put off by Ted's casualness with death.

"He died instantly, one shot. Look," he pointed to a wound in the side of the victim's neck. "The bullet entered here—blew most of his spine away. Didn't know what hit him. Can't find any other wounds. When can I move the body?"

"As soon as Sue Lawrence, our evidence tech, is done."

Ted gave Ray a tired look. He hated waiting while the police gathered evidence. He wanted to go home and get back to bed.

3

~~~~

Sheriff Elkins was leaning against his patrol car and drinking coffee from a large, insulated cup and dreaming about a cigarette when Deputy Lawrence drove up the two-track to the Holden cottage.

"Sorry I'm late," she said as she climbed out of her car. "I couldn't get back to sleep after I got home. I finally fell asleep just about the time the alarm clock went off."

"I just got here a few minutes ago myself. Let's start on the porch," Ray responded, leading the way to the front of the cottage; Sue noticed he was carrying a wooden stake and some string. He pushed the screen door open and held it for Sue. He pointed toward the broken window and the screen behind it. "We have the hole in the screen and the slug over here in the wall, and they seem to be in line with where the victim was standing." Ray's inflection suggested a question.

"Yes, I don't think the bullet was deflected much."

"So let's run a string between those two points and we can sort of eyeball where the shooter was." He put a tack in the wall just below a circle that marked where the bullet was buried, attached the string to the tack, and ran the string to the hole in the screen.

"Take this stake out to that dune. I'll yell to you where I want you to put it."

Sue walked in the direction of the beach; when she got to the top of the dune near the water, she turned back and faced the cottage. As Ray gestured, she moved the stake until he yelled, "Right there." She pushed the stake into the sand. Ray walked out to join her.

"The shooter was probably no more then five feet one way or the other," said Ray. "See a shell casing anywhere?"

"No, I was looking for it as I walked out here; I didn't want to push it into the sand."

"Let's work our way out from this point in each direction, some automatics throw the brass a pretty good distance."

They covered the area three times without finding anything, the third time using a rake Ray brought from the cottage.

"It's not here. What do you think?" asked Sue.

"The shooter either picked up the shell, which would have been difficult in the dark, or he used a bolt action rifle. Then he ran for his car that he left…"

Sue finished his sentence, "Behind one of those unoccupied cottages down the way."

"Let's see how long it would take," said Ray.

They headed across the dune at a brisk pace. When they got to the first cottage Ray checked his watch.

"How long?" asked Sue.

"Less than three minutes."

"And if he was running," she opined, "he could have cut that in half."

"Even in the dark and rain?"

"Well, maybe two minutes," she offered with a smile. "Then another minute or two to the highway, and he's gone. How long before Jake got here?"

"I'd have to check the log to tell you accurately, but I think about fifteen minutes."

"So even if the shooter took a leisurely stroll out, he would have had five or ten minutes lead on the first unit, and…"

"And what?" asked Ray.

"Well, we're assuming that the killer had a car parked here, and that's how he escaped. But we have no evidence to that fact. He might have walked out, had a car hidden on one of the old fire roads a mile or two from here. Or he might have come by boat."

"That's all true. I guess it depends on who the killer was."

"What are you getting at?" she asked.

"The shooter was very skilled. If this was done by a professional, he would have come to the area to do the job and gotten out fast. I doubt if he would have taken the time to learn the terrain well enough to find out where all these little roads in the woods go. And I doubt if he would have taken the time to arrange for a boat. The most efficient thing to do would be to stake out the victim for a few days, get a sense of his habits, and then devise a plan to do the killing and get away safely."

"So you think this was professional hit."

"Might be. We'll know more when we get additional information on the victim."

"Is there anything else you want me to do here, Sheriff?"

"Go over the area again with a metal detector, just in case the brass is buried in the sand. Later today or tomorrow I want to bring the victim's wife back here for questioning. I want you to be here for that. Also, see if any of those cottages are occupied. Then cover the drives and two tracks on foot just to make sure the shooter didn't drop anything."

"Given the lack of physical evidence, where do we go from here?" she asked.

"We question the witnesses again, check for any evidence that we might have missed, dig the bullet out of wall and send it to the State Police Lab, and see if there is any information on the victim on LEIN and NCIC."

"And what happens if we don't find anything new?"

Ray could tell from Sue's expression what she had just come to realize.

"Since you have been on the force—this is your third homicide, isn't it?"

"That's right," she answered. "We had the deer hunter in November and the woman who shot her husband in late January or February."

"And those are fairly typical of the kinds of homicides that we see up here, only a few each year, and they are usually open and shut—you've got the body, the motive, and usually a killer who wants to make a statement."

"And this one?"

"It's too early to tell."

4

Marc was awakened by a loud banging on the back door. He noticed the sunlight framing the edges of the thick curtains, and he heard his dog, Grendel, drag his license and rabies tags drag against the floor, but it was clear that the dog was not going to investigate the noise.

Marc pulled on some worn, khaki shorts. As he walked down the hall to the kitchen, he could see a familiar face peering in the window next to the door. He opened the door.

"Why's everything locked? You're not in the city."

"Why are you getting me out of bed in the middle of the night?"

"Middle of the night, hell. 9:00 a.m. is the middle of the night for you summer people?"

Marc yawned, stretched, and rubbed his eyes several more times. Then he took a long look at his boyhood friend. He saw that Ray had less than a day's beard and he was wearing a tie, although loose, with the top button open. The uniform that covered his short and stocky frame still showed some evidence that it had once been pressed.

"Are you cleaning up your act?" asked Marc. "Even at this ungodly hour, you're more in uniform than I've ever seen you."

"Ungodly hour, it's midday for us working folk."

"I'm still impressed by the uniform. You spent years trying to effect the country-cop look, and now you're looking almost citified."

"Well, there is an election coming, and I thought it was time I started to improve the department's image a bit. Which leads me to the reason for my visit. Rumor has it you're becoming a local voter." When Ray talked, his whole face, round with a pointed nose, was mobile, and he punctuated his sentences by blinking and moving his head. His face had humor. He looked like a character in a Hogarth print, or one of Dickens' street urchins who had grown to middle age.

"The rumor is true, but campaigning at this time in the morning?" said Marc as he stretched again.

"You've got to catch the voters when you can," replied Ray with a sleepy smile. "The election is turning into a real horse race. I'll have to work this time if I want to stay in office."

"I thought you might have tired of the job by now. I'm surprised someone hasn't enticed you back downstate with a more challenging position."

"I've been up here for quite a while. It agrees with me. And," he continued with a mocking smile, "this job is worth keeping. It's one of the few jobs in the county with steady pay and a new car every year. Anyway, I was out this way and thought I'd stop and see if you were here yet."

"I arrived on Friday. Want some coffee?"

"Have I ever turned it down?" Ray stood in the doorway between the kitchen and the living room. "Place doesn't look any different than when your grandparents lived here. Did you move anything up with you?"

"Just my clothes, some books, two computers, and some small personal things; Elaine is keeping the house."

"She got the gold mine and you got..."

"Not really, she'd picked out everything in the house. It was all hers. She always ridiculed my taste. All I wanted were my personal things. I was happy to leave everything else. No use bringing baggage filled with unpleasant memories. She got the house, and I got the hound."

"Well you got the best part. Where is old Grendel?"

"He'll wander in when it looks like breakfast is in the offing. He doesn't feel he has to be a guard dog anymore." As Marc started the coffee maker, he looked over at his friend. "I'm glad to see you. What brings you out this way?"

"We had a murder last night, couple of miles from here on the big lake. The victim is from Chicago. I wish you summer people would keep that stuff downstate. It's not good for the tourist business. And it may not be good for this incumbent sheriff just before an election." Ray bounced his thumb off his chest several times.

"How so?" asked Marc.

"My opponent," he laughed, "will argue that the homicide rate has increased a hundred percent. He'll tell the voters crime is increasing here faster than in Detroit."

"So you're up to two?"

"Two so far this year. Let's hope you fudgies keep it under control for the rest of the season."

"Still take it black?"

"Think I've changed?"

"It's possible. You've been here for almost ten minutes and you haven't lit a cigarette."

"True. I stopped four or five months ago. It was time. It was real hard to quit. And every time I have a coffee or a beer, God, I'd like to have one."

Marc got two mugs and the coffeepot and carried them out to the deck. Ray followed. "So tell me about the murder?" he asked as they settled into deck chairs.

"The murder took place at one of those big old cottages on Otter Point. Place looks a lot like this, probably been in the family for years. Name's Holden, Randy Holden, he's from Chicago."

"Randy Holden," Marc repeated.

"You recognize the name?" Ray asked.

"I haven't thought about him in years."

"Was he a friend of..."

"Never a friend, just someone I knew. You might have met him, too."

"Name doesn't ring any bells. And he didn't look familiar."

"How did he die?"

"Bullet through the back of the neck. The kind of shot that deer hunters like. You don't waste any meat."

"Do you have the killer?"

"Don't have a clue. Holden and his wife were entertaining friends, had just come back from a play. The victim was mixing drinks. Shot must have been fired from the dune just off the water's edge. It was during that heavy thunderstorm we had about midnight. No one heard the shot. And no one saw or heard a car leaving the area." Ray sipped his coffee. "What do you remember about Holden?"

"Not very much. I met him up here when we were in high school. He was a friend of a friend—you know how that goes, especially when you're in high school. He was a friend of Mel Wallace. I think they went to Cranbrook. Mel's parents had a cottage in that area. He'd come by and visit Mel. Randy would also come to the parties Mel threw when his parents left him up here alone." Marc paused and drank some coffee. "And during my first two years at Michigan, he was in a couple of my classes. He lived in one of those old fraternity houses on Washtenaw near Hill Street. I would run into him from time to time or see him walking up South University, usually with an attractive girl." Marc paused.

"Anything else?"

"I ran into him again after I got back from the Navy. He was still living in the Detroit area. He had finished law school at

Wayne or U of D and was working for a group of personal injury lawyers. He told me he was making a mint suing General Motors. He and Mel were still hanging out together. I think I saw him three or four times the summer I got back. A year or two later Mel told me Randy got in trouble with the Michigan Bar over some of his cases."

"What did he do?"

"I can't remember the details anymore. It had something to do with a scam his firm was running. They were working with a thoracic surgeon. They would find older or retired workers from the General Motors foundries in Pontiac, Flint, Saginaw, and wherever else GM had foundries. The doctor would check them over and do the necessary diagnostic work to show that they had lung damage caused by their years in the foundry. His firm would bring suit against GM in Wayne County and win every time, splitting with the plaintiffs."

"So what was the scam?"

"I think they got sloppy. You might want to check on the details. But I think it was so easy that the doctor just started creating evidence without doing the tests, and Randy was going to court knowing that his cases were built on fabricated evidence. They finally got nailed for it. And there was a bit of humor in it."

"What was that?"

"It all came out just after the Jaycees named him one of Michigan's Outstanding Young Men."

"Did he get disbarred?" asked Ray.

"That I don't know. I know he left the state and moved to Chicago. I remember Mel telling me he bought a seat on the Mercantile Exchange and was making a killing in gold, or wheat, or pork bellies, or something. And I heard that he moved on to junk bonds. Mel said he had made big money for some rich clients and was getting rich himself by churning their accounts."

"What's that?" asked Ray.

"That's when you move your clients' money from stock to stock. With each trade you pocket a hefty commission. You can get by with churning in an up market, especially if you do your homework. You can still make money for your client. But it's not ethical, and you're really cheating them."

"Mr. Stockbroker, do I note some disapproval?" asked Ray in a teasing tone.

"Well, most of the people in the business are honest and work hard at serving their customers. Then there are people like Randy and that whole parcel of young kids with the high priced MBAs—the Harvard, Wharton, Stanford, Chicago group—those kids were making more in their second or third year of business than I was making after twenty years. They are so arrogant. They seem to think that they have a birthright to rape the system. It doesn't bother them that they're getting rich at someone else's expense."

"Do I detect some anger?"

"Yes, I think he was one of them," continued Marc. "I've seen a lot of them, and I think he was the type. I hate what they're doing to the business."

"Who would have wanted him dead?" asked Ray.

"Hard to tell. He might have fucked with the wrong person's investments. Call Mel, he lives in Grosse Pointe, has his law office in the Ren Cen. I'm sure he can tell you more. He might be able to give you the names of some people who would know about Randy's recent activities. Tell him you're a friend of mine." As he poured some more coffee he asked, "How's your love life?"

"I've been spending a lot of time with a new woman friend, a recent divorcee. She's our age, pleasant and interesting—got a condo on Lake Michigan. I've been staying with her part of the time.

"Living in sin during an election, how does that go down?"

"No problem: bunch of retired people, downstaters, in the condos who love having a police car in the parking lot. They're all good Republicans. I make a special point of telling them I'll personally check on their places when they're away." Ray finished his coffee, "Well, I better run and get cleaned up and shaved. The

TV crew will want an interview live from the scene. Thanks for the coffee. Glad you're back."

"When are we going fly fishing?"

"I can probably get loose a couple of hours tomorrow afternoon. The Hexagena hatch should be starting any day now. I'll bring the flies. I know you don't have any."

"When do I get to meet this new lady?"

"Soon. She's in Seattle now, daughter just had a baby—soon as she gets back. Tell your dog I was here to see him."

As Ray drove away Grendel wandered out onto the deck, slipped over the side, marked two corners, and climbed back up, wagging his tail and whining for breakfast.

5

Ray arranged to have Tawny Holden, the victim's wife, brought back to the scene for questioning. Sue Lawrence was sent to pick her up from the summer home of Larry and Jean James.

Ray got to the cottage half an hour early. He walked out to the beach and stood next to the stake they had pushed into the sand earlier. He closed his eyes and tried to visualize how the scene would have appeared to the shooter. He could see the porch, bright against the darkness of the stormy night. He visualized the people he had questioned and placed them on the porch. He thought about how the scene would have appeared through a telescopic site. He centered the cross hairs on the victim, felt the rifle kick, and watched the pandemonium on the porch, watched the people run into the cottage, watched the cottage go dark.

Then Ray headed down the beach to the cottages a few hundred yards south of the victim's. He thought about a car parked in the darkness. He walked along the two-track drives, sand surfaces washed clean and made smooth by the heavy rain. There were no tire tracks, just the impressions from another walker. Ray retraced his steps back along the road to the victim's drive.

He was just about to enter the cottage when Sue came up the drive. He walked to the passenger door and opened it for Tawny Holden. As she emerged, Ray was surprised by how tall she was; she had appeared so small and fragile when he had questioned her briefly the first time.

"I don't want to go back in there," Tawny said, gesturing toward the cottage. "Can we talk at the beach?"

They arranged themselves on three metal lawn chairs on the deck next to an old boathouse. Tawny took the chair in the center. Ray sat on one side and Sue on the other. Sue held a pad, preparing to take notes.

Ray asked, "When did you first meet Mr. Holden?"

"It was last October. He was on the afternoon flight from O'Hare to LAX. I'm a flight attendant for United. The plane was almost empty. There were only five or six people in the first class section, and most of them slept all the way. He was in an aisle seat in the first row, and I ended up talking with him on and off during the flight. After, he came up to me in front of the terminal. I was waiting for the employees' van. He asked if I wanted to have dinner. I got my car and came back and picked him up. We went to my place so I could change, then I took him to his hotel so he could check in. We went to a little restaurant on the beach, had a wonderful evening. He was a lot older than anyone I'd ever dated, but he was kind, and gentle, and funny. He was a nice change from the man I was seeing." She paused and looked out at the lake. She pulled her feet onto the chair and wrapped her arms around her legs. She was wearing a loose fitting linen suit, the whiteness of the material accented her deep, reddish-brown tan. Her long hair, pulled tight with a ribbon at the back of her head, dropped below her shoulders. "Perhaps I was on the rebound," she continued in an almost trance-like voice. "I'd been involved with a pilot. He was married. I was in love with him, but he wanted out. Randy came along when I needed someone."

"How much time passed between the time you met him and the time you saw him again?"

She looked out at the water for a long moment, then said, "We were sort of a couple from that evening on. I had expected it to be only a weekend stand, but I started staying with him when I had a layover in Chicago."

"How often was that?"

"At the time it was about two nights a week, but then I changed my schedule so I could spend long weekends with him. He had this wonderful apartment on Lake Shore Drive. After a couple of months he asked me to marry him. I wasn't excited about getting married, but he was most insistent, so I said 'yes.' We got married in front of a judge at the Cook County Court House. After, we went on a honeymoon in Tahiti."

"Did you know how he made his living?"

"I knew he was involved in stocks and bonds or some kind of investments, but nothing more than that."

"Did you know any of the people he worked with?"

"No. He did most of his work at home. He had a room filled with computers. He seldom went to his office, and I never went with him when he did."

"Did you meet many of your husband's associates or friends?"

"He would introduce me to people that we ran into at restaurants. And he did take me to a few parties, but I don't think I met anyone who he was close to."

"Do you know much about his life before he met you?"

"No, we didn't talk about the past."

"So you really don't know much about him."

"Not much, there was no reason to drag out our previous lives for examination. That's one of the things I really liked about Randy. He didn't need to know about my past."

"Is there something in your past that you wouldn't have wanted him to know about?"

"No, nothing that I'm embarrassed about or regret, but I don't think you understand my point. Most men want to know about your past. They want to know about your family, where you grew up, things like that. And they're usually curious as hell about other men you've dated. Randy didn't seem to need to know any of that stuff. He didn't want my history. And I didn't ask him about his life."

"Do you know if this was his first marriage?"

"He told me that he had been married twice before, and he didn't have any kids."

"And you weren't curious about the other two?"

"No, not really. After all, this is my third, and I'm a lot younger than he is, was… I was delighted to find someone who didn't seem interested in my past relationships. I'm a 'today' person, the past is past—you can't do anything about it, you can't change it."

"How about his family, did you meet any of them?"

"His parents are both dead. He only has a sister, and she doesn't talk to him. He told me it was because his parents left him this place. He said his parents knew his sister would never have the money to look after it properly, so they left it to him because they wanted it to stay in the family. Randy said that she would have sold it the instant she got it."

"Have you met her?"

"No."

"When did you come up here?"

"A week ago Wednesday. Randy wanted to show me the place, said he really loved it. I was ambivalent about coming here."

"Why?"

"He was asking me to take part in his past. I didn't want to do his history, but he insisted."

"What did you do when you got here, who did you see?"

"Until yesterday we spent the time by ourselves. We went shopping and out to eat, but we didn't get together with anyone. We were having a nice, relaxed time. I was starting to enjoy it." She reached back and put her hands around the large cord of blond hair, just where it emerged from the ribbon that held it together. She raised her hands over her head, lifting the hair. She dropped the hair back and stretched her arms out, slowly lowering them and wrapping them around her legs again. She pulled her arms tight. "But yesterday was awful."

"Yes," responded Ray, thinking that she was talking about the shooting.

"I was the odd one out. These people all go back a long way. They have this history together. I was the outsider. And I could tell the women resented me."

"Resented?" asked Ray.

"I'm twenty years their junior. They both have daughters my age—something they established early in the evening."

Ray thought she wasn't going anywhere and it was safe to pull the conversation back. "Did your husband ever tell you that he was in any kind of trouble or was afraid of anyone or anything?"

"Never. Everyone I met liked him. He had a real way with people. He was absolutely charming. He was good to me. He was considerate and generous. That's more than you get out of most relationships, isn't it, Sheriff?"

Sue looked up from her notepad. She gave Ray a long look.

"Do you know if your husband had a will?"

"We had one drawn up soon after we were married."

"And you are the sole beneficiary?"

"Yes."

"And you have seen the document?

Tawny looked irritated, "Yes, it's a joint will."

"Do you know the size of the estate?"

"No, I don't have any idea. He lived well, but I doubt if he was rich. You can tell."

"What do you mean?"

"I had the impression that he consumed what he made. I meet a lot of people. People with real wealth act differently. You can just tell. You're probing about his money—are you trying to determine if his estate is large enough to temp…" She looked directly at Ray. "Am I a suspect?"

"We have to explore all possibilities."

"Don't waste your time on me. He made me feel good, and loved, and happy. You can't buy that."

"What will you do now?" Ray asked.

"I still have my job. And I have a little house just off the beach in Venice. There's nothing here for me." She looked out at the water, seemingly lost in her own thoughts and then looked over at Ray. "What about the body?"

"The autopsy is being done today. It should be available tomorrow. Have you made burial plans?"

"Dr. James called Randy's lawyer in Detroit. The lawyer's going to contact his sister and see what she wants to do. I thought that maybe the family had a special burial plot or something."

"Will you stay in the area much longer?"

"I want to leave as soon as possible."

"Would you be willing to come back? I may need to talk to you again in the course of the investigation."

"Sheriff, I want you to get his killer."

6

When Ray returned to his office in the early evening, he found Sue Lawrence working at a computer. As he approached, she looked up and said, "I'm just finishing cleaning up my notes on your interview with Mrs. Holden. I'll be able to print you a copy in a few minutes."

"What did you think of Tawny?" Ray asked.

"An interesting woman. She's only a few years older than me, but she's decades ahead of me in experience. When I brought her over this morning, she didn't have a lot to say, but on the way back to Suttons Bay she was more relaxed and talkative."

"Did you learn anything new?"

"Nothing new. The things she said just reinforced her answers during the interview. She makes it clear that the past is past. She also told me that this was the second violent death of someone close to her in the last year."

"Who was…"

"Another flight attendant, a women she shared a house with. The accident took place on the ground, one plane was taxiing, the other taking off. I sort of remember seeing it on the news. As I was editing this report, I was wondering how much events like this shape the way you look at the world."

"Hard to say," responded Ray. "As you reread the interview, does she sound credible?"

"I think so, but it's hard for me to say. Her life is so different than mine. It's hard for me to put myself in her head."

"Do you think that she had any reason to want her husband dead?"

"If she had, it wasn't suggested by anything she said during the interview. But," she hesitated for several seconds, "I worry about being too naive, too accepting. She might be a skilled actress and I don't see through the act."

"But your gut level response?"

"I think she's real."

"Let's say she was involved. What might her motive be to have him killed?" asked Ray.

Sue smiled at him. "You like to hear other people try to figure things out, don't you?"

"I do. It helps me think about them, and I like the way you work. I worry about being too cynical. Anyway, back to the motive question."

"There's the question of the estate, but that will only be an issue if she's heir to a lot of money. And that's something you can check on fairly quickly. From what she said, I don't think that she thought he had a lot of money. Another thing, I don't think she cares about those things."

"Support." said Ray.

"Well, I helped her pack. We took things out of drawers and off hangers and folded them. She has nice things. They're all fairly new. Everything is of good quality, but there was nothing really expensive. I don't think she cares about things that much, and I doubt if she is overly concerned about money. It doesn't seem that important to her."

"How about another man, what if she wanted to get out of this relationship? What if this pilot she mentioned wanted her back?"

"I don't think so. First, this was a new relationship and it seemed to be working. Second," Sue held up two fingers, "she's a strong character. She's able to direct her life. If she suddenly wanted out, she would have walked. Let me turn the tables: what did you think?"

"I was a bit bothered by her lack of affect. But I agree, it doesn't look like she had anything to do with the murder."

"Doesn't leave us with much."

Ray nodded agreement. "I'll have you do some checking. We'll see if Holden has a criminal record or any current legal problems. I'll check with his lawyer and see if I can get information on his estate. I'll look through the house again. Tomorrow, I'd like you to do the same. Take a lot of time. I didn't find anything, but you might see something I missed. And carefully dig that slug out of the wall. We'll send it to Lansing and see if we can learn anything about the weapon that was used. These kinds of investigations take on a life of their own. Sometimes when things look completely hopeless, you get a big break. We just need to keep plugging away."

7

Lisa Alworth, a portable phone tucked in her pocket, carried her lunch—a plate in one hand, a tall glass of ice tea in the other—from the kitchen at the back of the cottage, through the living room, and out to the front porch, turning as she backed through the screen door. The midday sun burned directly above.

She set the plate and glass on a small rattan table at the side of lounge chair and, before sitting, spread suntan oil on her face and bare arms and legs. She settled on the lounge, glanced at her watch, and picked up the phone. She briefly looked out at the lake and then began keying a number 011-44-...After a few distant-sounding clicks, the phone began to ring with the distinctive sound of the English phone system. Beep-beep...beep-beep...beep-beep...beep-beep...beep-beep.

"77046."

"Hello, Mother."

"Lisa. How are you?"

"Fine. I was just about to hang up."

"We've just got in. I heard the phone ringing as I came through the door."

"Out gallivanting, huh?"

"Elliott needed some peat for the garden, and I wanted to get some fresh fish for dinner. We went to Port Isaac. Place was jammed. Since the tourist season has arrived, it's quite impossible to get around. And how are things in your part of the world?"

"I'm sitting on the front porch. It's hot, high eighties. The lake level is up a bit this year. We've lost about ten feet of beach."

"And the cottage, any damage over the winter?"

"I had some trouble getting the pump started. Jon came over and fixed it. Something electrical. Other than that everything seems to be working."

"And how are you?" Lisa could hear concern in her mother's voice.

"I'm fine, Mother."

"Are you sure?"

"Yes."

"And you're not lonely?"

"Not at all. I've been playing tennis every morning with Kelly; she's up with the kids. Last night I had dinner with the Fredericks. I'm as busy as I want to be. And guess who arrived last week?"

"Who?"

"Marc."

"Marc? He hasn't been up in years. How long is he going to stay?"

"I haven't talked to him yet, but the rumor is that he's divorced, and he's quit his job…"

"You're kidding,"

"And he's permanently up here, at least that's the story."

"You sound very pleased. You always were sort of sweet on him, even though…"

"Even though what, Mother."

"You know, his, his…"

"Age? Having trouble saying the "A" word?"

"Well, there is that."

"And how much older was father?"

"Let me think, about the same, but…"

"But what?"

"You're an incurable romantic. So am I. And you know how much I've always adored Marc. I was so disappointed when he married that horrid... What's her name?"

"Elaine."

"Yes, that's right, Elaine. What he ever..." there was a long pause. "Elaine is quite beautiful, and very bright, but not someone I'd ever want to spend time with."

"I thought I'd drop by and see Marc. Maybe this afternoon."

"Lisa, go slowly. Divorced men are at loose ends for a while. But I agree, Marc is very special. I can see why you're attracted to him. You know I never disliked your Chris, but Marc is...is much more substantial, there's more...well I better shut up before I get myself in trouble."

"So you won't be shocked if I start dating Marc."

"Oh, Lisa, not shocked. You know that. It just takes me a while to get used to things. And when you see him, give him my love."

"I'll do that."

"And stay in touch, dear. I'll try you this weekend."

They said their good-byes and Lisa put the phone on the table. She had a gentle smile on her face as she picked up the iced tea and gazed far out into the lake.

Marc sat on the floor of the living room unpacking boxes of books and sorting them into stacks. He had planned to do this earlier, but the day had been hot and he found excuses to work outside.

A knock at the screen door on the front porch interrupted his concentration. The brilliant sun, reflecting off the lake, streamed in around the person centered in and framed by the doorway. A figure, female, looked in at him. Marc tried to make out the silhouette.

"Hi, are you receiving visitors?" a not unfamiliar voice inquired.

"Come on in," Marc replied, squinting to see the visitor. "Is it little Lisa?"

"Little Lisa, no. Little Lisa grew up years ago," she replied with a sarcastic laugh. "It's thirty-something Lisa."

As she moved away from the sun's glare, Marc could see her clearly. "I guess it was a while ago. You know how it is with summer memories. Somehow I expect everything up here to be frozen in time. Do you want something to drink? I've got iced tea and beer."

"I'll have the tea. Don't get up, I'll get it."

"It's in a pitcher in the fridge, and there are glasses in the drying rack." Marc watched as she walked to the kitchen. She was very tan, and in profile, very thin, thinner than he remembered. His memories of Lisa were of short hair, but now she was wearing it past her shoulders in the ordered chaos of current fashion.

"Do you want some?" she called.

"No, I'm still working on a warm beer."

When she returned to the living room, she settled in an overstuffed chair, rolling her legs under her.

"Is your mother here?" Marc asked.

"No, she and my stepfather are in Cornwall. They bought an old mill on the coast near Tintagel that they're fixing up. I don't think they are planning to come back to the States until Thanksgiving."

"Michigan not exotic enough?"

"It's not her idea; you know how much she loves it here. But Elliot wants a place that's theirs together, not something left over from an earlier marriage. Actually, I think it's romantic. She sends her regards."

"I was looking forward to seeing her," said Marc. "She was a big sister to me while I was growing up."

"And your baby sitter."

"And my baby sitter. The only one I can really remember. I think my grandparents had her around almost permanently the first few summers I was with them. Her job was to keep me occupied during the day. Most of the time Ray Elkins was here, too. She had to look after the two of us. I bet that wasn't an easy job.

"Later, your mother and I became good friends. She was just enough older that I always looked on her as an adult, but I really cared about her in a little boy way—you know how school boys sometimes fall for their teacher." Marc tore the tape off the bottom of the box he had just emptied, flattened it, and tossed it onto a pile near the door. "I was really unhappy the summer she got married. I was jealous of the guy that took my buddy away. And before long she had her own baby to sit." He pulled the tape off the top of another box, gazed at Lisa, and smiled. "You look terrific. I don't think I've seen you since the summer you got married. Let's hear about you."

"I'm good, and you probably know I'm not married."

"I heard there were problems, but I didn't know. How long?"

"Almost two years. It was clear we wanted different things, and I saw no point in extending the agony. Chris has remarried; they have a new baby. I think that's what he wanted all along—something conventional. I was too much of a career woman."

"Was the divorce painful?"

"Painful," Lisa looked thoughtful. "No, just disappointing. I consider it a starter marriage." Lisa gave him a teasing smile. He liked the smile, relaxed, confident, without tension.

"Still in advertising?" asked Marc.

"I've taken six months leave of absence. I've had the money Dad left me sitting in a savings account for years. I'm probably chasing ghosts, but I want to spend a summer up here like I did as a kid. I want to see if I can be that happy again." Lisa looked pensive. Then her expression shifted. "Enough of me, you're the one with the big breaking news. Big time stock analyst leaves prestigious Wall Street firm and wife and runs away to the woods."

"You better get the headlines right. Wife of stock analyst finds true happiness with her psychiatrist."

Lisa looked uncomfortable. "I didn't know. I'm sorry if I was sounding insensitive."

"You weren't. The marriage had been over for years. But I never seemed to overcome inertia and get out."

"Why not?"

"Well," continued Marc, "inaction is often the easiest course. She had her life and I had mine. I would leave for the city early and come back in the evening, often very late. Elaine had her career, her friends, her schedule. So there wasn't much of a marriage, or even a friendship. I thought there should be more to a relationship, but I wasn't sure. And most of the time I was too busy to give a damn. The psychiatrist did me a great service. But I'm not here because of the breakup."

"You're on sabbatical?"

"No. One day I knew I had to get out. I had a friend die of a heart attack, and a few months later another friend died of cancer. I thought—what the hell am I doing here? I moved East because Elaine didn't think she could survive anywhere besides New York. The rest of the country was too provincial. I never really liked it there. But after a while I stayed on because I didn't think the firm or the financial world could get along without me. We kid ourselves into believing that we're indispensable. So to make a long story short, I decided I wanted to be some place that I loved."

Lisa laughed. "We're just like the locals, unemployed or retired. I'm unemployed and you've retired…"

"But I'm not retired. I'm going to set up my computers in the study and be active in the market. Only this time I'll be spending my time tending my own investments."

"I'll let you get back to your unpacking. I've got to meet someone for tennis. Can we get together tomorrow?"

"How about dinner?"

"Is this a date?" she asked in a playful tone.

"Date—I don't know how to date. Let's just have dinner."

"You're on," she laughed. "Oh, almost forgot. Ray Elkins came by a few days ago. He was looking for my mother. He asked if I knew when you were going to get here. You won't recognize your old friend."

"He was here this morning. He caught me sleeping in."

"Did you notice the 'new' Ray?"

"I was surprised that he has stopped smoking."

"He's working hard at developing a new image. Not only has he stopped smoking, he shaves daily, wears a tie most of the time, and sometimes his uniform is pressed. And he's even getting his patrol car washed. All the things that he took pleasure in shedding when he left his college job and moved back up here."

"Why the sudden change?"

"He's got some real competition in the election this time. He wants me to be his media advisor for the campaign." She looked at her watch. "I'm going to be late. I'll tell you more about it when I see you tomorrow. I'll pick you up. When should I come by?"

"Is six okay?"

"That will be wonderful. See you then."

Marc watched her go. He leaned back against the overstuffed couch and drank the last swallow of warm beer from the bottle. He liked the old summer house, the smell of the forest coming in through the open windows, the sound of the wind moving in the trees, the sound of the waves on the beach, the smell of sun tan oil on a pretty woman—the memory of an old summer feeling came back briefly.

8

~~~~~~~

L isa gave Marc a teasing smile. "Do you want me to drop you off in front of the restaurant?"

"No, I think that I can hobble in from the parking lot. But I am thankful that you drove—good eyesight, solid reflexes and all. You kids have it all over us old guys. Doubt if we'd have made it otherwise."

"You're just not used to being picked up for a date."

"I can't imagine being on a date, picked-up or otherwise. And this isn't a date," grumbled Marc as he tried to mask his obvious enjoyment of their sparring.

"If it isn't a date, what is it?"

"Two summer people—old family friends from different generations—going out to dinner." He glanced at her quickly. "What would your mother say if she thought we were going out on a date?"

"Well," said Lisa, "first, she would tell me what a cute little boy you were. Then she would tell me to be careful with recently divorced men because they don't know where they are for a year or two. And then she'd wish me good luck. She is a real romantic."

"Doesn't sound like her."

"Doesn't it?" Lisa looked across at him with a mischievous grin. "Well, she called this morning. That's what she said when I told her we were going to dinner. She sends her love." She reached for the door handle and paused. "Let's walk a few minutes before we go in," she said as she slid out of the car.

"Should you put the top up?"

"No, it's not supposed to rain until late tonight."

They walked to the pier and out on the breakwater, an arm-like structure of huge, limestone boulders that reached into the lake to protect the harbor. They stood and looked out onto the lake. The sun was still high on the horizon, its path reflected in the waves. The glare made them squint as they looked west to the Manitou Islands. Below the sun they could see the outlines of dark-gray thunderheads moving across the water from the Wisconsin shore. They turned and looked toward the village: boats jammed the harbor, every slip in the marina was filled, and several large boats were tied up in the deep channel along the sea wall.

"I can't believe how much this place has changed," said Marc. "When I was a kid this was a real fishing village with five or six trawlers anchored in the river, smoke houses, nets on drying racks. The sea wall only protected the opening of the river. There wasn't a marina, just a ramp where you could launch a boat. And there was an old World War II landing craft you could take if you wanted to go out to the islands. Now look at the place."

"The buildings are still picturesque, and from out here they don't look too different. And they do look better than your average boutiques and fudge shops," Lisa offered.

"But that was real. This is all so damn phony: overpriced and sentimental watercolors with nautical themes, Indian jewelry made in Taiwan, beaded belts from Hong Kong, even the Mexican jumping beans are probably from Paraguay, or Peru."

"You're really doing your best to sound like an old curmudgeon. Enough of this talk about what was. I'm hungry, and I get cranky when I'm not fed on time." She took Marc's arm and led him back off the sea wall, across the pier and past the shops to the restaurant. Although he protested a bit in the process, he was enjoying the playful way she was pulling him along. Their table, as Marc had specified when he made the reservation, was next to a large window overlooking the harbor. A waiter appeared with a bottle of champagne as soon as they were seated. He showed Marc the label, opened the bottle, and poured a partial glass for his approval. The waiter then filled both their glasses.

After he left the table, Lisa lifted the bottle from the ice. "How did you know?"

"Your mother told me—I guess I forgot to tell you. She called this morning. Must've called me after she called you. She's worried about you being up here all alone. Asked if I'd look in on you occasionally."

"And she just happened to mention which brand of champagne I prefer?"

"As a matter of fact, she said you told her we were going to dinner this evening, and I asked what you liked to drink..."

"Did you talk very long?" she interrupted.

"We had a lot of catching up to do, and she was in a talkative mood. I think she's a bit homesick."

"Yes," said Lisa, "I sensed the same thing. This place is special. It's hard not to be here in the summer."

Marc lifted his glass: "Let's hope our memories of this summer are as rich as those that brought us back."

Lisa brought her glass to his. Their eyes met. Marc looked a bit embarrassed. He launched into a conversation. "Ray called this afternoon. He was intent on reaching you and got no answer at your place."

"He caught up with me just before I left to pick you up," said Lisa. "He wants me to watch his interviews on the news. He thinks that with my background in advertising and public relations I can help him make better use of the media, especially now with this murder investigation getting him some TV exposure."

"I've seen many strange things in my life, but I never thought I would see someone package Ray. I can't imagine he would have trouble winning an election."

"Well, it is the first time he has really been challenged, and by one of his former deputies—someone he fired for incompetence. The guy's name is Hammer, Todd Hammer. He's running a tough campaign and getting a lot of support from the gun lobby because Ray's been leading a group of police organizations that are trying to get the legislature to ban the sale of assault rifles."

"But Ray has been sheriff for years, seems like he knows most of the natives and lots of the summer people."

"I don't think there's a chance that he will lose the election," said Lisa. "But Hammer has really gotten under his skin. Ray told me he had a difficult time firing him—I guess it was quite ugly. But the thing that burns Ray is that Hammer spends his evenings making the rounds of the local bars, telling the patrons that Ray is soft on crime and wants to take their guns away. And he gives out bumper stickers that say *Sack the Wimp, Hire a Hammer.*

"Does he get any takers?"

"I guess he gets some; I have seen a few of the stickers on old pickups. Ray says there are a lot of rednecks around here who are terrified that they might lose their guns. The really popular bumper sticker with this group is 'My wife, yes; my dog, maybe; my gun, never.' I can't imagine why any woman would ride in a car with that sticker on it." She paused and looked at the menu. "Enough politics, what are you going to have?"

"What's good?" asked Marc.

"The white fish is wonderful. And they have steaks, chops, the usual stuff, but you should be watching your cholesterol—given your age and all." She smiled mischievously.

"My God, you sound like a…" He didn't complete the sentence "Besides, my cholesterol is extremely low."

9

~~~~~~~

Lisa parked next to Marc's cottage and switched off the engine. "Want me to walk you to the door?"

"I expect it. Remember, I'm old fashioned."

When they got to the door Marc turned and asked, "Do you want to come in for a nightcap?"

"Sure," said Lisa.

Marc opened the door and switched on the kitchen light. Grendel, lying in front of the stove, raised his head slightly and thumped his tail against the floor.

"Come on old man, time to go outside."

"How old is Grendel?"

"Fifteen. He has really started to show his age. Watch. He'll be back at the door in two minutes. In the old days he would stay out and explore all night if he could. Now his only joys seem to be sleeping and eating. What would you like?"

"What are my choices?"

"Let me check." Marc started going through a collection of bottles in a cupboard. "There's half a bottle of tolerably good cognac, some Armagnac, a Portuguese brandy that looks like its been here for years, some anisette and a few things of uncertain origin."

"Not a bad stock considering you just moved in."

"This stuff has been here for years—aged in woods. What will it be?"

"The cognac."

He poured the liquor into two snifters, let the dog in, and led Lisa into the living room. "Would you rather sit on the porch?"

"I think it's getting too cool. Besides I've always liked this room." Lisa settled into the large sofa. "Are you going to redecorate?"

"I guess I should," he replied, handing her a snifter and sitting down near her. "Most of this stuff goes back to the thirties and forties. Some of it dates from the time my grandparents built the place. I really like it this way, but Elaine would tell you I know nothing about decorating."

Lisa lifted her glass, took a small sip, and said, "That almost sounded like hurt, like you still care about what she might think."

"I don't. It was always a sore point with us. One of the reasons she gave for hating to come up here was that she found the decor, to use her phrase, 'distasteful.' She referred to it as 'Roy Rogers Rustic.'"

"Are you really through the divorce, or are you still hurting?"

"As I told you yesterday, the marriage had been over for years. And I'm glad she forced the issue by getting involved with her shrink. But in a funny way I think I was a bit hurt. No one wants to be the one who is left, regardless of how bad the situation. Maybe my pride was hurt. Perhaps I felt bad because someone else could make her happy when I couldn't. It's all pretty irrational stuff."

"You can't work through these things in a rational way," agreed Lisa. "I was the one who asked for the divorce, and I was elated when it was final. But then, six months later when I heard he had remarried, I was absolutely crushed. For some absurd reason I felt our marriage should have been important enough that he would have remained in mourning for a suitable time. Have you dated—excuse me, you don't date—have you seen other women since the divorce?"

"I had dinner a few times with people from the office. And some of my colleagues—female colleagues—tried to fix me up or invited me to those embarrassing dinner parties where you figure out immediately who you're being paired with. Nothing serious, I didn't leave anyone behind. And you?"

"Right after the divorce I dated a lot of different men. But I never found anyone I wanted to be serious about."

"Want some more cognac?" Marc picked up the bottle.

Lisa shook her head. "What I really would like to do is take you to bed." She pulled his face to hers and kissed him. She slowly ran her tongue back and forth across his lips. "And I promise I'll still respect you in the morning," she said with a playful laugh.

"What would your mother think?"

"Your baby sitter would approve."

The storm woke Marc about 2:00 a.m. He got up and closed the windows and went back to a warm bed.

10

～～～

S oon after the Coast Guard issued a small craft advisory, the little harbor was jammed with boats seeking shelter from the storm. The cold front, sweeping down from Canada and across Lake Michigan, moved faster than expected, reaching the eastern shore just after dark. At its leading edge was a sharp squall line with high, gusty winds. This was followed by hours of heavy rain, lightning, and thunder.

Boaters, many coming out of the storm in yellow, foul weather gear, filled the restaurants and bars in the harbor. The ferocity of the storm added to the intensity of the partying. Sometime after 2:00 a.m., the merrymakers were pushed out into the raging storm. The rain, falling in sheets, pounded the parking lots and marina; whitecaps crashed over the sea wall. Lightning flashed in the green-gray sky; the earth shook as the thunder reached the ground.

Just after 3:00, south of the village, a transformer was hit by lightning. It crashed to the ground in a pool of burning oil. The village, marina, and surrounding countryside sank into darkness, darkness occasionally shattered by flashes of lightning.

A shadowy form moved along the docks. Gasoline spilled across the deck of a large sailboat.

A sharp explosion rocked the harbor. Then a massive bolt of lightning, attracted by a tall shaft of aluminum, shot to earth. The charge ran along the mast and guide wires, over the deck, and into the water. A wave of flames exploded across the boat; burning fuel covered the water. Several explosions followed the first as the fire spread across the water and along the docks.

11

Before retiring, Ray had opened the curtains so he could watch the lightning, but he quickly fell asleep, a sleep not disturbed by the romp of wind, rain, lightning, and thunder. The metallic ring of the phone, however, jarred him back to consciousness.

"Sheriff, better get down to the marina. There's a bad fire."

"Fire? What's burning?"

"Jake said boats, docks, fuel on the water; it's real bad. And the power is out—there's no light. The fire department's there, but things are out of control. I've requested help from the other departments, foam truck is coming from Traverse City."

"Get all our people there and work on back-up. How about medical?"

"There's a unit at the scene, and I've got several more coming. Mercy Flight is standing by and a Coast Guard chopper is on the way.

"Keep me informed," said Ray.

As he raced toward the lake, Ray was struck by the darkness: no lights in buildings, no yard lights, no street lights in the village, only the beams of his headlights cutting into and being diffused by the heavy mist.

He was still miles away when he first saw the glare on the horizon. As he drove closer he could see the flames rising from the harbor, then reflecting back from the ceiling of low clouds. As he approached the marina, he saw the flames on the water, running along the docks, shooting up from burning boats. He could see the shadowy silhouettes of fire fighters on the shore. Behind them, on a rise at the side of the marina, was a throng of spectators, their faces lit by the glow.

Fire hoses carrying water from the river to the two pumpers blocked the drive to the marina. As soon as he emerged from his car, Ray could feel the intense heat. Acrid smoke burned his nose and throat as he ran toward the shore.

Ray found Jake next to the first truck. "I think we've got everyone off the boats. Bernie says all they can do now is contain the fire and let it burn out."

"Injuries?"

"Nothing much yet, just minor stuff. God only knows what we'll find in the morning."

Ray spent the remaining hours of darkness coordinating the efforts of the emergency services. By first light, a shelter had been established in the township hall just across the road from the marina. By 8:00 coffee and food were being served to the fire and police crews, and the people who had been staying at the marina.

Initially everyone seemed to be accounted for. Then Sue Lawrence brought Ray a tall, lean, graying man wearing only a bathing suit.

"Ray, this is Stuart Baker. I want you to hear what he saw."

As he started to tell Ray his story, Sue brought Baker a blanket and put it over his shoulders.

"I was still on the Wisconsin side of the lake when I first heard the storm warnings. I was coming over from Green Bay to Old Mission. The wind came up real fast, so I thought I might as well run for the Michigan shore as try to tack back to Wisconsin.

I was able to keep all the sails up for a while, but when the storm got really intense, I just used a storm jib and the auxiliary engine. It must have been well after two when I came into harbor. The place was dark. I was able to tie up just inside the sea wall. I heated up a can of hash and was having a sip of whiskey before going to sleep when this explosion scared the hell out of me. I crawled on deck and the whole place was on fire..."

Ray motioned with his hand, a sweeping gesture. "The whole place?"

"Not at first," Baker said. "When I got on deck a big sailboat in the slip across from me was completely engulfed, and there was burning fuel on the water all around it. Within a few seconds the cabin cruiser next to it was on fire. I saw two people get off it just before it exploded, pouring a lot more fuel into the water. Then it really spread fast. As I looked back at the sailboat, I saw a figure climb out of the cabin. His clothes were on fire. He staggered to the side of the boat and jumped in. He just disappeared; I didn't see him surface." He paused.

"What else did you see?" asked Ray.

"Not much more. I decided it was time to get the hell out of there. I spent seven summers building this boat, and I wasn't gonna let it go up in flames. I started the engine and backed into the channel and went out into the big lake. A couple other boats made it out behind me. I ran along the shore a few hundred yards until I got pushed onto a sand bar. I was stuck tight. I just sat there and watched the fire. I swam in a little while ago to see if I could get someone to help free my boat."

Ray thanked Baker for his help, and Sue got an address and phone number. By mid-morning the victims of the fire had been questioned. Ray and Sue listened to many more stories about the panic and chaos that followed the initial explosion and fire, but no one else had seen the burning figure. Several people provided the name of the owner of the large sailboat. They believed he was staying alone on the boat.

An arson investigator from the state fire marshal's office and the two state police divers arrived in the early afternoon. The divers carefully worked their way across the marina. They checked the submerged remains of the boats. Then they checked the deeper areas of the marina and the adjoining river.

In the deepest part of the channel, near the entrance to the harbor, the divers found a body entangled in weeds. The divers brought the body to shore, and Ray watched as it was loaded on a stretcher. He knelt down and closely inspected the badly burned remains. Sue was at his side. He glanced over at her. She looked green. He began to dictate into a small recorder. "Male, presumably Caucasian. Entire body has been burned; skin deeply charred in areas, especially face, hands, and chest. Deep lacerations on right thigh, chest, right arm, probably from propeller blades. Right hand severed and missing."

The divers returned to area where they had found the body to look for the hand. A further search of that area and the marina failed to produce it.

12

◡◡◡

Ray turned off the pavement onto the two-track, parallel trails of sand and mud the width of a car with grass growing between them. It already was late afternoon. The sun— high, breaking through gaps in the tight ceiling of leaves, running to earth in incandescent columns of heavy, moist air—created a dappled effect on the fern-covered forest floor. Ray was tired. His clothes smelled of smoke. As he made the final turn, he noticed Lisa's car next to Marc's. Finding the screen door to the kitchen was latched, he walked around to the front. Marc was on the deck, leaning back in a chair, feet against the railing, looking out at the water. He stopped and watched. Marc was obviously lost in thought.

"Have I caught you at a particularly pensive moment?" he asked.

Marc, startled, looked over at the intruder. "You look like hell. Where have you been?"

"Haven't you been watching the news?"

"No, slept in. I've had a real lazy day. And the TV doesn't work, must be twenty or more years old. What did I miss?"

"Probably the biggest story in years. We even made it to national news."

"What happened?"

"Did you hear the storm last night?"

"Yes, it woke me once."

"Well, it appears that lightning hit the mast of one of the larger sailboats in the marina—boat exploded. There was a fuel fire and several other boats burned to the water line."

"People hurt?"

"Bumps and bruises, a few minor burns, and three or four fire fighters went to the hospital for smoke inhalation. Burning fiberglass and plastic are pretty vile stuff. And there is at least one death. We recovered a badly burned body. I think it's the man who was on the sailboat."

"When did this all happen?"

"Sometime after three."

"How long did it take to get the fire under control?"

"Didn't ever really get it under control, just contained it and let it take its course. They're not equipped to fight that kind of fire."

"Lisa and I were there for dinner last evening."

"I noticed the car," said Ray referring to the presence of Lisa's car.

"You wouldn't have expected anything like that." Marc ignored Ray's last comment.

The screen door slammed. Lisa had just emerged, hair wet, smelling of soap and shampoo, wearing one of Marc's Oxford cloth shirts and a pair of tan shorts—the fit suggested that they were also borrowed. She carried a tray with sandwiches and two glasses of tea. She greeted Ray. "You look like hell. Did we have another rough night in the jack pine jungle?"

"He was just telling me that a sailboat was hit by lightning in the marina. There was a hell of a fire."

"Anyone killed?"

"One fatality. I hope that's all."

"We're having a late lunch. Do you want a sandwich or something to drink."

"I can only stay a minute. I have to get a shower before we do a press briefing. There's a chamber concert at the Colony tonight. Are you people interested?"

"Do you know the program?" asked Marc.

"Schubert, Op. 100, and Mozart. Faculty members from Interlochen; they're good."

Marc looked over at Lisa. She nodded. "We'd like to do that."

"Let's meet there, just in case I get held up. I'll take care of the tickets. Pick yours up at the box office."

"We'll give you a late supper after the concert," said Lisa.

"That would be great. Make sure you watch the 6:00 news. See you tonight."

Lisa and Marc sat in silence for a few minutes until they heard the engine.

"Do you think we shocked him?" asked Marc.

"Hardly. I don't think Ray is easily shocked, but you're a bit embarrassed, aren't you? I saw you blush when I came out of the cottage," said Lisa, showing some obvious joy at needling him. "Has Ray always been interested in chamber music?"

"He was in love with a cellist when he was in graduate school. She was on the music faculty and part of a very successful string quartet. I think that she was Ray's first real love, but she ended up marrying someone else."

"And then? I don't really know much about Ray other than his life up here."

"He accepted a job teaching criminal justice, fell in love with another musician, and they lived together for a number of years. She got some very aggressive kind of cancer and died. I saw him a few months after her passing. He was a basket case. But by then he was a department chair and it looked like he was going to spend his career at the university." Marc paused for a long moment. "When he found out his mother was terminally ill, he took a leave of absence and came back to care for her. About that time the sheriff announced his retirement and some locals wanted Ray to run in the primary. He called me, asking what I thought about the possible career change. I said if he really wanted to live up north and would be happy in that job, he should go for it. After he won the primary and general election, he resigned his university appointment. And the rest, as they say, is history. A footnote to the story: When I saw Ray boldly make that change, I realized that I could do it, also. It just took me a few more years."

13

Ray was not looking forward to interviewing the ex-wife of the dead man. He arrived a few minutes before the time the person on the phone had said, "Mrs. Bussey will find it convenient to meet with you then."

A pretty young woman, probably the voice on the phone, met him at the door and escorted him through the living room and out onto a deck overlooking the lake. By her dress it was difficult to tell whether she was a maid or a secretary, but her formal manner suggested she was not a family member. She offered him a chair at an umbrella-covered table and said Mrs. Bussey would be with him in a few minutes.

Ray surveyed the house, large and new, a kind of rustic-modern that mixed stone, wood, and glass. A glass-walled living room faced the lake; the vaulted ceiling rose two stories. The house was perched high on a hill over the water, and the deck was cantilevered out over the side of the hill, providing an extraordinary view of the lake and shoreline. The deck was an elaborate piece of craftsmanship—redwood, cut and fitted in an intricate pattern, a Jacuzzi carefully worked into the pattern at one end of the porch.

Ray's attention was pulled back as the sliding door opened and a woman emerged. The young woman who had met him at the door followed her, carrying a tray with coffee.

The woman crossed the deck to where he was sitting, extending a hand as she approached. He rose to greet her. Her hand was cold and bony, her grip strong. "Please stay seated. I'm Rachel Bussey." She seated herself across from Ray. The tray with a silver coffee pot, creamer, sugar bowl, and two cups—thin, white, and translucent—was placed on the table. The young woman silently departed.

"Sheriff Ray Elkins, ma'am. I just have a few questions. I know this probably isn't an easy time." He looked across the table. She was wearing a large pair of dark glasses and he couldn't see her eyes. She was very slim, almost frail, and appeared to be in her early forties. Her hair, very blond, was pulled into a tight roll at the back of her head, giving the impression that the hair was helping to pull the skin taut over her narrow, tense face. She was wearing a dark blue cotton skirt, a pink knit polo shirt, and white court shoes.

"I'm upset," she said in a low voice, "but hardly grieving." Without asking whether or not he would have any, she poured two cups of coffee and served one to Ray. "Cream and sugar?"

"No, this is fine."

"We've been divorced for almost three years—had this place built just before he wanted the divorce. Our old cottage was in the village, a cute Victorian my great-grandparents built around the turn of the century. But he wanted something that reflected us, the house we were going to grow old in together, and before it was finished he wanted a divorce." She paused, pulled a cigarette from a pack and lit it. "What can I help you with?"

"Now that the body has been recovered and identified, we need to know who to contact regarding its disposition."

"You should probably notify his brother Sidney, Sidney Bussey. He lives in Kenilworth and has an office in Evanston. I imagine he'll take care of things."

"Are there any children?"

"We had one, died in infancy. No other children."

"At this time," said Ray, "we believe Mr. Bussey was on the boat alone. Would you know if there might have been other people on the boat?" He sensed her immediate tension after he asked the question.

"For a while he kept an airhead on the boat. He went public with the little bitch before the divorce was final. But I haven't seen her this summer. The last two summers I seemed to run into them every time I was in the village. If she was on board, so much the better. God got them both. I don't know why he had to keep the boat here after the divorce. I think he did it just to spite me. When he was a high school boy he used to spend his summers around here. Then his parents bought a place in Harbor Springs—I don't know why he didn't go back there. He's more the Harbor Springs type. And that boat—we had a smaller one before the divorce—he bought it to just to show me what he was doing with our money. He knew that I'd notice that the biggest boat in the harbor was his."

"I don't quite follow you." Ray was surprised at the direction the conversation was going.

"Arthur had a need to show his money, if you know what I mean. His family always gave the appearance that they were well to do, but it was only after we were married that I found out how close to the edge they were. He made his fortune with my family's money. And I have to admit we did well by him."

"What type of business was Mr. Bussey in?"

"Investments, all types. We were married when we were seniors at Northwestern, and then he got his M.B.A. at Chicago while I taught elementary school in Winnetka. After he got out of school my father lent him enough money to get started. He was a real promoter and had the knack of buying up vacant land a year or two before the urban sprawl moved in that direction. Then he moved into developing malls. I knew he was leveraged to the hilt, and that a lot of his business was little better than gambling, but he always seemed to pull it off—even though I was amazed that he could get banks to lend him money. I remember asking him if he ever thought about the people who sometimes lost their life savings when one of these schemes collapsed. He said there was no problem, the government would take care of them. I guess we're all paying now."

"You said you were divorced three years ago."

"Three years last May. He wasn't as difficult as I thought he would be. But then, I had the best law firm in Chicago, old family friends. The only things he wanted to haggle over were the Bears' tickets."

"Bears' tickets?" repeated Ray with a restrained, quizzical smile.

"Bears, Chicago Bears, four season tickets on the fifty-yard line, thirty rows up. They had been in my family since the thirties. I made damn sure he wasn't going to get to sit there, sit there with his bimbo, where my grandfather and father once sat. I told my lawyer to tell him to go to hell."

"I know this has to be unpleasant, but might I call on you again if I need further help?" Ray asked.

"Yes, certainly. I'll be here until October."

"Thank you for your assistance, and the coffee." Ray rose and shook her hand. "I can find my way out."

Ray paused at the door, looked out at the lake. He could make out the silhouette of a distant ore carrier steaming north to the Straits. From that height he could see the earth's curve across the horizon and the long lines of waves moving toward shore— there was a sense of rhythm and harmony in the scene.

14

Lisa and Marc waited for Ray outside the hall until an usher insisted that the concert was about to begin. Lisa saw Ray slide into a chair near the back between the third and fourth movements of the Schubert. He joined them at intermission.

After the concert they walked across the road to a coffee shop.

"I hated to be late, but I had something to take care of. I really liked the Schubert. Kubric used it as the theme music in Barry Lyndon."

"I remember that," said Marc.

Lisa nodded her head, "Must have been before my time."

"Kids," said Marc, "high culture is lost on them."

"But we do understand the use of media. Do you want a critique of your interview on the six o'clock news?" she asked Ray.

"Yes, I'd like that."

"Well, I don't know about the hat," she said with a broad smile letting him know that what was to follow wasn't a serious observation. "It makes you look a bit like Smokey the Bear. Initially, I thought I was watching a report on the dangers of forest fires. It was only when I saw the marina in the background that I realized that you were talking about last night's fire." Then, modulating her voice to suggest the serious nature of her comments, she continued, "Actually, you projected a convincing image of intelligence and competence…"

"Come on, Lisa," interrupted Marc, "it was more than image. Perhaps it wasn't image at all. You've got the real person, intelligent and competent, explaining what happened in a clear and thorough fashion—thorough given that we only had a sound bite."

"You're really bothered by the idea of packaging, aren't you?" Lisa asked. "You mentioned it at dinner last night."

"I really am. I'm bothered by the fact that the packaging is more important than the content. It's like the label on the side of a potato chips bag that says the product is sold by weight, not by volume. Translation, 'Don't be surprised if the bag is half-empty.' I am tired of elected officials who are half-empty—the top half."

"Now, Marc," launched Lisa, "just because I am in the business doesn't mean I like or approve of the way media is used to package politicians. Take Ray as an example," she paused and put an arm on Ray's shoulder. "His media image is important. It's important that people know that he is bright and competent. If he weren't projecting those qualities, it would be important for us to help him make those qualities apparent to the viewers. Fortunately, he does all the right things quite naturally."

Lisa turned to Ray. "Can you tell us about the victim? You were careful to say as little as possible on air 'pending notification of next to kin.'"

"As I said in the interview, the divers found the body. It was caught in some weeds at the bottom of the channel. Wasn't a very pretty picture. The body was badly burned, with some deep lacerations from boat props. And his right hand was severed at the wrist. We didn't recover the hand."

"Could you identify the body?" asked Marc.

"We had a pretty good idea right from the start. The guy who manages the marina, Jack Harris, told us who owned the boat; he thought the victim had been around most of the day. And the people whose boats were moored near his said they had seen him on the boat in the evening. Once we got the body out of the water, Jack and a couple of other people identified him."

"So you're having a problem finding family members to notify?" asked Lisa.

"Earlier we were, but I finally got hold of his brother in Chicago before I came over here. Wasn't able to reach him until this evening—hate to give bad news by phone, but what can you do?"

"So the victim had no one in this area?" asked Lisa.

"Well, he did, and didn't. His ex-wife lives in this gorgeous summer home on the top of Peach Bluff. I went up to see her first, and she gave me the victim's brother's name."

Lisa asked, "Did you have to break the news to her?"

"No, I think she knew when I called. Most of the people around the marina knew. He was the only one not accounted for. Anyway, she's a bitter woman. There was no sadness over his death, just hate and anger—not so much in what she said, you could just feel it. She told me the divorce took place three years ago, but given the anger, you'd a thought it took place yesterday. She indicated that 'another woman' was involved. She referred to this other woman as the 'little airhead,' the 'little bitch,' and the 'bimbo.' At the time, the terms seemed out of context because the rest of Mrs. Bussey's speech was very formal, very correct."

"Now that we have the marital history," said Lisa, "who was the victim?"

"Man's name is Arthur Bussey, lived in Lake Forest, Illinois. He was about our age." Ray made a gesture indicating he was talking about Marc and himself. "His wife said he'd been summering here since he was a kid. Strange that I'm asking the same question two days in a row... Did you know him?"

"Arthur Bussey," thought Marc, "Arthur Bussey, doesn't ring a bell. Did he have blonde hair?"

"Didn't you all?" asked Ray rhetorically, lifting his eyebrows and showing teeth with a sarcastic grin. "But certainly not the last time I saw him."

"Oh, Ray," exclaimed Lisa.

"Arthur Bussey," continued Marc, letting the last exchange pass. "No, the name is not familiar, and I'm reasonably good at names. If you had a picture—any old picture from when I might have known him—perhaps I would remember the face. Do you remember him?"

"No, but all you city boys looked alike, dressed alike…"

"We're back to the 'townies vs. the fudgies?' What's happening with the murder case? This fire has really pushed it to page two," said Marc.

"So much the better, I wish it would push it off the back page. Other than the slug, which we've sent to Lansing, we have no physical evidence. Have you met Sue, my evidence person?" Marc and Lisa shook their heads. "She's really bright and very thorough. She's gone over the area with a fine tooth comb and hasn't found anything."

"Has his wife been able to provide any help?" asked Lisa.

"I just had one conversation with her, but I don't think she knows anything—you can usually tell right away. They've only been married a few months. Seems to know little about his business, and hardly knows his family or friends."

"How about the other people there that night?" Marc questioned.

"I think they were there by chance. One of the men was an old fraternity brother, the other someone Randy knew at Cranbrook. They usually get together once or twice a summer to play golf. Both told me they had given up trying to pin him down on exactly what business he was in. They said he seemed to enjoy making it sort of mysterious—like it wasn't quite legal. This doesn't leave us with much."

"So, what do you do now?" asked Marc.

"I'll talk to the wife again, and probably to the other two couples who witnessed the shooting. And I've requested data on the victim from the state and national information networks we use. I hope we get some useful information from these sources. But

I've worked on cases before where you don't have much, and you don't ever get much."

"What do you do then?" asked Lisa.

"About all we can do is investigate every lead, collect and preserve any physical evidence. You try not to lose track of the case, but that sometimes happens when there are no further developments. If this turns out to be the work of a hired killer, the case may never be solved."

"Never solved?" Lisa looked incredulous.

"Never. I don't know what the exact figures are on contract killings, but it's fewer than ten percent. You can't connect the killer through any motive, and, if he's a competent professional, when the job is done he's gone without leaving any evidence to tie him to the crime. In the cities you never notice this because these murders make the news and then are crowded out by the next day's gruesome happenings. Arrests for this type of crime are few and far between. Non-arrests don't make the news."

"How do you go about arranging—contracting—for a murder?" asked Lisa.

"I think it's quite informal, but people with the right connections know how to get all sorts of things done. From what I've been told, the arrangements for a job like this are usually done at a great distance so the source of the contract can't be traced. And the successful hit men are known for being dependable. In this case the killer most likely drove into the area and checked into the Hilton. The guy probably looks like a middle-aged businessman, not the kind of hoods you see in the movies. He plays eighteen holes at the Bear everyday, talks and dresses like everyone else at the Hilton. He would take time to study his victim and develop a plan to do the job and get away. One shot—the victim's spine was blown away—the right professional, the right tools, the right outcome."

"The right outcome for whom?" asked Lisa.

15

The remains of the large sailboat lay on the concrete parking lot in the marina. Mike Ogden, the arson investigator, was waiting for Ray by the side of the boat. The keel and bottom of the boat were a soft blue. A ribbon of white, smeared with oil and blackened in places, marked where the water line had once been. The deck area was a mass of charred and melted fiberglass.

"Did you find anything unusual?" Ray asked.

"Unusual?" said Mike, a stocky redhead in his early thirties. "For us, the whole damn thing is unusual. We spend most of our time investigating businesses that have been torched, usually by their owners. Occasionally we get something a bit more interesting like an arson-murder. I can only remember doing a couple of powerboats, but never a sailboat. This is terrific."

"So what did you find?"

"Well, as you can see, the top of the boat is pretty well destroyed. Let me show you the mast first." Mike led him over to the mast that lay in another part of the parking lot.

"The bottom's pretty well charred up, but from the top you can see it's been melted by the lightning, must a been one hell of a charge. Looks like someone used a gigantic arc welder on parts of it. Now look at this," he said pointing to a stainless steel collar that had cables attached to it. "I don't know anything about sailboats, suspect these parts all have names, but look how the cables are welded to these rings. Some of the charge must have followed these cables to ground. There are other interesting things. Look at this." He pointed to a small engine near the rear of the boat.

"That must be the auxiliary engine," said Ray. "What's so interesting about that?"

"Look closely. It's a diesel. Cute little thing, isn't it?"

"So what's your point?"

"No point," said Mike. "Not yet, anyway. I'm just trying to figure out what happened, the order of events. The other boat fires I've worked on were caused by a buildup of gasoline fumes in the bilge. They're usually ignited by an electrical spark, like from a faulty plug wire, when the engine is started. So my original theory was that the mast took the hit. In the process of the charge going to ground, the fumes in the bilge exploded and gas from the boat's tank fueled the fire. But diesel fuel isn't very volatile, so you're not going to have an explosion of diesel fumes. And there's something else that's interesting."

"What's that?"

"I don't know if you want to crawl in and get all messed up. You can see part of it from here." He pointed into the cabin; most of its roof had been burned away. "You can see a burn pattern."

"What does that mean?" asked Ray.

"You can see where a burning liquid flowed into the cabin. Looks like the stuff came through the door and ran to the lowest areas of the interior. You can tell from the size of the burn pattern that there was a substantial quantity of fuel."

"You think that it was diesel?"

"No, the stuff was a lot more volatile. It had to be gasoline."

"So what do you think happened?"

"It doesn't all quite fit, but then things seldom do. I would guess that the lightning hit the mast, and the charge came down the mast and those steel cables. There must have been a container with gasoline near one of them that exploded when it got hit by the current. He probably had a tank for an outboard. Don't most of these big boats carry a dinghy or an inflatable?"

"I suspect they do," said Ray.

"So," continued Mike getting into his role as a raconteur. "This guy's sleeping, see. He's probably had a few. We found some gin bottles in there. This storm blows in. The lightning hits the mast and then a gas can blows, spilling burning gasoline onto the deck and into the cabin. The victim wakes up and the whole damn place is on fire. He manages to get out of the cabin and dives for the safety of the water. And that's all she wrote."

"What would have been the victim's condition?"

"The autopsy will show that his lungs are singed. I'm surprised that he made it off the boat."

"And you don't think that there's any sign of foul play."

"Not unless you've got a murderer who can direct lightning. I think this can be labeled an act of God or an accident caused by nature, depending on the way you choose to explain the unexplainable. But there is one thing that's less than kosher that you might want to look into."

"What's that?"

"Come over to the truck?"

Ray followed him.

Mike opened the back doors and took out a plastic package. He unwrapped it carefully.

"I'm trying to be very gentle. I don't know if this got hot enough to become unstable. We found this tucked off to the side with some tools in the engine compartment."

"Is it what I think it is?" asked Ray.

"Eight sticks of dynamite. If I had known what it was, I wouldn't have pulled it out of the boat. I'd have called Lansing and let one of our resident nuts come and extract it. They're coming to pick it up. If this stuff had gone, you would have had a lot more casualties." Mike continued on with obvious sarcasm, "I'm not into the yachting scene, but is this a common cargo?"

"I'll have to check," said Ray. "It might be the newest thing among the white wine and Brie crowd."

"One more thing, Sheriff."

"What's that?"

"Could you call Lansing and say you need me at least until Labor Day?"

"Don't you want to stay until the end of deer season?"

"No, saw *Bambi* three times; don't do that kind of thing."

16

Deputy Sue Lawrence met Tawny Holden at the airport and drove her back to the cottage. Tawny made one last sweep through the cottage, gathering a few remaining personal possessions.

"Thank you for coming in with me," she said to Sue. "I didn't want to be here alone."

"Are you worried about your safety?" asked Sue.

"Not at all, but this place," she paused and slowly looked around, "is full of bad memories." Tawny's voice took on a business-like tone. "I think I've got everything."

"Are you going to keep the cottage?"

"Keep it?" Tawny gave Sue a look of incredulity. "No. I don't want to ever come here again."

Sue glanced about her, "There are so many beautiful things, don't you want any of them?"

"No," said Tawny, "they don't mean anything to me. They're part of someone else's life. I don't want anything that will remind me of what happened."

"What will happen to the house?"

"I talked to Randy's lawyer at the funeral. He will look after getting rid of the place; his sister might be interested in it. Randy once told me that she wanted it. I think the fact that he got the place when their parents died had a lot to do with their falling out. I guess they hadn't talked in several years, and I had never met her before Randy's funeral, but she was very nice. The James' called her after Randy was killed. They drove me downstate for the funeral and invited me to stay with them, but she insisted that I stay with her. She handled all the arrangements for the funeral. I was a complete basket case."

"What are you going to do now?" asked Sue.

"I'll go on just like before. I'm scheduled to work next week. I just need to get on with my life."

"Don't you have family or someone that you can fall back on for support?"

"No family to speak of. My father died when I was little, and I never got on with my mom. I left home as soon as I graduated from high school. I haven't made any effort to keep in contact, and my mom hasn't either. I don't believe in keeping relationships going that do more harm than good."

As Sue was locking the cottage, Ray came up the drive. She stopped and waited. "Do you want to go into the cottage?" she asked after he emerged from his car.

"Not really. I do want to talk with Mrs. Holden for a few minutes."

"Can we sit at the beach, Sheriff?" Tawny asked. She motioned toward the cottage, "I've said my last good-byes to the place. I'd rather not go back in."

"I'd prefer it," said Ray.

They settled into the three metal lawn chairs facing the water.

"It is beautiful here," said Ray looking out at the lake.

"Yes," agreed Tawny. "I'm a beach and water person. My place in California is only a block from the ocean."

Ray looked at her as she was talking. Her rich tan and sun-bleached hair confirmed her love of the beach. But as he looked at her attractive face, he sensed her pain. He couldn't exactly tell what gave him the impression, but she seemed terribly worn for her years.

"I know the last few days have been very difficult for you," he began, "but I was wondering if you had any more thoughts about who might have wanted your husband dead?"

"I spent a lot of time thinking about that, Sheriff. Do you use visualization?"

"Visualization? I don't quite follow you."

"I was trying to think about the past given what has happened. I tried to visualize conversations Randy and I had; I tried to see if I could put another interpretation to things. I also tried to remember the phone calls I'd overheard; was there anything I might have missed?" She paused and looked at the lake.

"And," prodded Ray

"I don't think I missed anything. If Randy thought someone was out to kill him, he didn't give me a hint that it was going on. The hard part about this is admitting to myself that I didn't really know him very well. It's strange—you meet someone, you get involved, you share your life, you share your body, but that doesn't mean you really know them. I don't think I'm naive, but I took everything that he told me at face value. You meet lots of men in my kind of work, you can usually spot the hustlers a mile away. They're incredibly obvious, although they seem to think that they are unusually subtle. Randy was sweet, he was kind to me, and he wanted more than my body for a night or two. I have no misgivings; he was clearly no saint, but he was better to me than any other man I've known."

Ray waited for a few moments, then said, "I appreciate the thinking you've done. What are you going to do now?"

"Go back to L.A. I'll stop in Chicago and pick up some things at Randy's apartment that I want. I wish I didn't have to do that."

"Because?"

"I don't like dealing with ghosts. I just want to get this all behind me."

"Whenever you're ready, Sue will take you to the airport."

"Thanks, Sheriff. I appreciate it."

17

~~~~

Ray saw Sue come into the front office and motioned her into his office with a sweeping gesture of his arm. She settled into a chair across from his desk.

"What did you think?"

"About?"

"About Tawny?"

"Well, Ray, I feel uncomfortable hazarding a guess. You've had so much more experience in this kind of thing."

"And you," said Ray, "are unusually insightful. Do you think that she is involved?"

"No, my intuition and all my logic say she's not."

"Why? Remember sociopaths are usually skilled actors."

"I know, but they are often so skilled that you can't help but be suspicious. I think she's real; I don't think she was involved in any way." Sue looked directly at Ray. "But I can tell that something is bothering you."

"I'm bothered by the lack of any affect. She is so totally controlled. Do you think that she loved him?"

"Love? I don't know. She's been married three times, and she's only in her late twenties. She really opened up on the way back to the airport; I think she needed to talk. She told me that Randy was the first man who was ever kind to her. So to answer your question, I think she loved him as much as it was safe for her to love him."

"What else did you learn?" questioned Ray.

"She got married the first time at eighteen; she married her high school sweetheart as a way of getting out of the house. They moved to L.A. and only managed to stay together for a few months. She worked and went to college for several years and then got a job with the airline. Her second husband, a pilot, was dashing and very romantic before they were married, but soon proved to be cruel and abusive. She stayed with him less than a year. Between marriages she had a number of other relationships, but nothing ever worked out. She said that she had just about given up on the possibility of a successful relationship when she met Randy, and this one, from the beginning, just felt right."

"It all sounds pretty grim," said Ray. "But let's be cautious. Verify her employment history with the airline and see if you can substantiate her account of her marriages. Let's hope her exes are alive and well."

As she opened a notebook Sue said, "I do have a couple of additional things for you."

"Okay."

"The man at the state police lab says the bullet is a steel jacketed 30.06, and it was fired from a Winchester model 25. McGee, that's the guy's name, says that was a very popular model, there were more than a million produced. He also said that the bullet is in pretty good condition. If we find the murder weapon, he's sure he could do a comparison that would stand up in court. And..." She turned several more pages, "I have a little information on Holden."

"What's that?"

"I took the information you gave me about Holden's possible problem with the state bar, the things your friend told you. I called my mother—this is using the good old girl network. One of her partners in the law firm used to be on the license review board. The man remembered Holden's case. He said Holden should have been disbarred, but a deal was worked out."

"What kind of deal?"

"It seems that Holden's dad was a former president of the state bar, and there was a lot of discomfort with pulling his license. The deal was that if Holden would agree not to practice in Michigan for a minimum of ten years, they would take no formal action against him."

"He plea bargained his license."

"That's what it amounts to. There's more. I got this from NCIC. Holden was under investigation by the SEC for violations of security laws, but no charges had been filed. Also, he had several civil suits brought against him in recent years by dissatisfied clients."

"What happened with those?"

"They were settled out of court."

"He sounds like a perfectly wonderful human being, doesn't he?" said Ray. "One of the disturbing things you discover in this business is that people who are clever and reasonably affluent can operate for years beyond the edge of the law and get away with it. And some poor bastard who steals a rusty old car…"

"Gets sent to Jackson," Sue completed his sentence.

18

Jack Grochoski had wanted to be in the military when he graduated from Fordson High in Dearborn, but his uncle got him a foundry job at Fords (as they say in Dearborn). He worked there until a long strike, came north for deer season, and then decided never to return to River Rouge. He built a small cabin south of Empire: fished, hunted, trapped, and eventually became the evening bartender at the Last Chance. During one long winter, he and the owner—more out of loneliness than any real attraction—were lovers. Later, Marge married a car dealer from Kalkaska and sold Jack the Last Chance.

Jack stood behind the bar washing glasses and surveying the afternoon customers. The bar had changed little in his years there. The knotty cedar on the walls had darkened with age, the color change apparent when old beer signs were taken down, and an A-frame entrance covered with shake shingles had been added in the 60s when A-frames were the fashion. At that time Jack also had the floor redone with vinyl tile in a pattern of red and black. The pattern was now barely distinguishable and the tiles were worn through to the concrete slab around the entrance and in front of the restroom doors. When the original chairs, chrome tubing with plastic covered seats and backs, started falling apart, Jack replaced them with oak chairs he bought when the furniture from the Methodist church in Nessen City was auctioned off, its congregation having moved away or died.

Some of the regulars from his earliest days were still around. Jack sometimes wondered how they could stand to sit on the same stool in the same bar year after year—and then would remember that he stood at the same place behind the bar year after year. There was a certain constancy that he enjoyed: the same faces, the same drinks, the same stories and jokes. And when one of the old timers died, he was reminded of his own mortality and the fact that the years were slipping by.

In the winters he would spend the afternoons and evenings with three or four of the regulars, old timers, who would make a beer last an hour as they smoked, talked, or peered at the TV that was always running above the bar.

In the summer, like this early July afternoon, Jack was always busy. The locals held down the right side of the bar and the tables near the pool table. The summer people liked the area near the windows where they could get a glimpse of the lake. The regulars drank beer, the old brands, from long-necked bottles—sometimes with a shot of blended whiskey. This hadn't changed in more than thirty years. The summer people drank light beer, gin with tonic or bitter lemon, and white wine. Jack remembered that in the old days—for the most part these were the children of the summer people he had served earlier—their parents and grandparents had drunk martinis, Manhattans, Scotch, bourbon, and tap beer.

The left end of the bar, near the TV, was usually occupied by Roger Grimstock. He was there every afternoon and evening through most of July and August and had been for years. Roger had frequented the Last Chance, first as a minor, standing in the parking lot at night trying to get someone to buy for him, and then as a college boy bringing in the other summer kids. In the winter he brought his fraternity brothers up between semesters for skiing and weeklong drunks.

Jack had never liked Roger. At first he didn't like him because he was afraid that the kid would get him in trouble with the liquor commission. Later, Jack didn't like his nasty manner. Roger would show up in the early afternoon, and like some of the locals, start with shots-and-beers, and then continue on with beers, sometimes until closing. The regulars had learned long ago to stay clear of him. He was always unpleasant, always looking for a row.

This Saturday Roger's pattern was the same as always. He arrived before 2:00 p.m., quickly had two shots-and-beers and settled into an afternoon of drinking and smoking. Jack moved with the rhythm of the bar, filling orders, chatting, listening to the stories of patrons. He usually wasn't given to introspection or to considering the interior worlds of his customers. This day, however, as Jack slid a fresh pack of cigarettes across the bar, he tried to remember what Roger had looked like in those early years. He closed his eyes for a long second: skinny, tow-headed, with light skin and bright blue eyes. Looking again across the bar it was hard to see the kid in this man—his eyes were pale and watery; his face, soft, and swollen like a dead animal; his flesh forming layers of bulges under his knit shirt.

Jack wondered what Roger thought about during those long hours, hours spent smoking and looking across at the bottles behind the bar or occasionally at the TV set. Why did he come to a public place if he wanted to be left alone? Why didn't he stay at his cottage and drink?

19

The rain, little more than a light mist for most of the evening, had become a steady shower. Roger Grimstock swore as he got to the car. He got a towel from the trunk and dried the driver's seat, then dragged the top from behind the seats and struggled to secure it to the windshield. He pulled the choke out and turned the key; the old engine sputtered to life. After lighting a cigarette, he sat for a few minutes and let the engine warm up.

He drove east about a mile and then headed south on Ely road. The rain intensified; his wipers—old, hard, and cracked— left the windshield badly streaked; the dim, yellow headlamps— generator driven—weakly reached into the rain and fog.

He slowed. Even in his alcohol-dulled state, he sensed something. At first he couldn't tell what it was. But as he began to climb a long hill, he became aware of the sound of another engine over the noise of the old sports car. He felt it behind him, but there were no lights. He accelerated; the sound of the other engine intensified. He clutched to down shift. The pitch of the other motor increased. Lights came on behind, high, over the cab, not on the fenders. He heard the bellow of the big V8 behind him. He accelerated. The gap closed.

Roger crested the hill. He hit the switch and the overdrive kicked in. On the long descent he started to pull away. He could see the other vehicle slowly falling back, but as he started climbing, the gap narrowed again. He switched off the overdrive. As the revs dropped, he pulled the car into third. The engine bellowed. The needle on the tachometer was well into the yellow. The truck pulled closer.

The lights of the truck disappeared just as the snowplow blade hit his rear bumper. He held on for control. He jammed the accelerator to the floor. He started to pull away from the truck, first by only inches, then the gap gradually widened. He looked at the dash. The needle was in the red; the engine screamed. Then there was a loud metallic explosion and a half-second of silence before the car started to spin. The wheels caught in the soft shoulder and the car rolled, side-to-side, down a steep embankment until it struck a large oak tree. The wreckage tumbled forward end to end until the vehicle came to rest, top down, in a rain-swelled swamp.

The truck on the road above stopped and backed onto the shoulder. A figure emerged, walked to the side of the road, looked down into the darkness, listened, and after several minutes got back into the truck and drove away.

20

~~~~

Marc was tense; he had been tense from the moment he awakened shortly after five a.m., rushing to shower and dress so he could drive Lisa to the airport in time for a 7:00 a.m. flight.

They stood in the departure area and drank black coffee from paper cups. At last her flight was called and as they walked toward the gate she said, "Remember to pick me up on Wednesday." She kissed him warmly and, without looking back, headed toward the boarding gate. He watched her go through the door, watched until he couldn't see her anymore. Then he went to the window and watched her walk across the tarmac to the aircraft and climb up the stairs.

As Marc walked back to his car, he felt down—lonely, sad, and angry. He had finally gotten used to the idea that Lisa had moved in with him. Now she was leaving for a few days to take part in the wedding of a friend. She had invited him to come along, but he wasn't comfortable with the idea.

Marc drove through Traverse City along the bay and then took the highway that ran along the shoreline to Suttons Bay. He stopped for breakfast at a small restaurant overlooking the water.

He tried to interest himself in the *Detroit Free Press* as he ate, but couldn't concentrate. He searched for the cause of his anxiety. Was he upset that Lisa was going to be gone for a few days, or was he feeling anxious that things had moved too quickly and he wasn't in control? Perhaps it was good, he thought, that he would have time to think things over. He left a half-eaten breakfast and barely-read paper and, still tense when he got back to the cottage, decided to take a long bike ride. As an adolescent he discovered that he did his best thinking on a bicycle.

Marc carried his bike, top tube resting on his shoulder, from the cottage out to the paving; he didn't like rolling it through the wet sand of the two-track. He rode south at Burdickville, went west at Fowler Road, and south again at Indian Hill Road. He used roads that he knew from long experience would be lightly traveled.

Marc was thinking about Lisa. He was trying to think about what he was feeling. An old acquaintance, but a relative stranger, had suddenly been living with him in complete intimacy. He was not used to the closeness. He tried to remember if he and Elaine had ever shared such relaxed intimacy.

He remembered the feelings—certain strong emotions—of years ago. But those weren't feelings he had ever had for Elaine.

Lisa had rekindled feelings that had once scared him so much. And, he thought again, it was moving too fast. He was not used to being close to anyone or letting anyone close.

He worked his way along the back roads until he got to Crystal Lake and Beulah. After twenty miles of hard riding and some difficult hills, he was starting to feel better. Nothing was resolved, but he was less tense. He stopped in Beulah for a Coke. The girl at the refreshment stand—probably fifteen or sixteen—he thought, also offered to fill his water bottles. He watched as she rinsed them and took the time to fill them with small ice cubes before she topped them with water. She was tan, blond, and had a bright smile.

Marc walked to the beach and sat on a cement wall to rest and finish his drink. A warm breeze filled sails far out on the lake and the July sun burned high in a cloudless sky.

On the area of beach nearest him, a group of teenage girls in two-piece suits—bright pinks, greens, blues, and oranges hiding and highlighting their barely concealed parts—were stretched out on towels, listening to music and sunning. Boys with cars crept back and forth on the road just behind the narrow beach, surveying the scene in a kind of motorized mating frenzy: windows open, arms hanging out, sunglass covered eyes fixed on the nubile forms. The village's police officer, parked on the opposite side of the street, leaned against his car and gazed out at the lake through mirrored glasses. His presence prevented any overt display of testosterone-induced behavior—there were no roars from the minimally muffled engines or squeals from the tires rolling on the blistering blacktop.

Farther down the beach, families were bathing, picnicking, and building sand castles. Just beyond the swimming area a trio of novice sailboarders bobbed in the waves. Occasionally one would manage to stand on the board and pull the sail from the water, only to be dumped into the surf again as the board leaped forward.

Marc finished his drink and started the long ride back. He took Cinder Road south of Honor, then Ely north. As his fatigue increased, the hills seemed to get longer and steeper. Near the top of one hill, a large black dog came charging out of the tall grass on the side of the road with a bellowing attack bark. Knowing he was too tired to outrun the dog, he stopped and prepared to defend himself with a water bottle and frame pump. The dog—tall, bone-thin, with long face hair like an untrimmed terrier—stopped his charge and approached meekly, whimpering and finally gently licking Marc's outstretched hand. His curiosity met, the dog turned and ambled down the road.

The adrenaline generated by this encounter gave Marc a new burst of energy, and he rode several more miles before stopping to adjust the rear derailleur at the foot of another long hill. That done, he sat on the side of the road resting and drinking water, his legs pushed out in front of him on the steep embankment. He was hot and tired; he felt like stretching out and dozing in the shadow of the hill.

His attention was suddenly attracted by the glint of something shiny in the tall grass of the swamp below. He looked again, but could not make out what the object was.

He carefully worked his way down the gravel and clay embankment, the hard soles of his bike shoes making the descent more difficult. He cut through the tall grass and ferns until he reached what looked like a new path, at the end of which he could see the object that first caught his attention, the chromed end of a tailpipe. He could also see four tires turned to the sky and part of a badly smashed trunk. He worked his way forward over the partially flooded swamp on clumps of grass and decaying logs until he reached the car. It had settled into the muck and only the bottom third of the car was above water. The door on the passenger side was sprung open. He kneeled carefully on the remnants of an old birch log and tried to look into the car. His view was limited, but he thought he saw what might be a body. He pulled at the door, but it was too mired in mud to move. He decided not to look again.

Marc retraced his steps, this time taking less care to find dry footing. He scrambled up the embankment, retrieving his bike on the way. A mile up the road he came across a Consumers Power truck; the driver was sitting on the tailgate eating his lunch. After Marc told him what he had found, the man called his dispatcher and asked that the sheriff be notified. He then drove Marc back to the scene and waited with him until the first sheriff car arrived.

Ray arrived a few minutes later and surveyed the scene. Marc stayed above while Ray and the deputy, after pulling on rubber boots, made their way to the car.

When Ray came back up the hill, Marc asked, "Someone in there?"

Ray nodded, "I'm afraid so."

"How are you going to get the car out of there?"

"We'll have to get a small bulldozer with a winch. It's going to be a while before the equipment gets here. I can have someone run you home," Ray offered.

"No, I am trying to work some things out—I need to do more miles."

Ray sensed Marc's anxiety and gave a knowing nod. He watched as Marc started climbing the long hill, standing, leaning forward, pulling the bike from side to side with each forward thrust.

21

~~~

Gawkers, a dozen or so, stood on the side of the road watching the activity below. Some of them had just been passing by and were attracted by the emergency vehicles. The remainder—people who sit at home and listen to police scanners, people who seem to be driven by a morbid interest in the misfortunes of others—rushed to the scene. Deputies by the side of the road prevented them from going down to the wreck.

The bulldozer operator, Ronnie Toole (known locally as Little Tarzan), in jeans, a sleeveless denim jacket, and no shirt, carefully backed his rig off the trailer. He followed an old fire lane from the highway and then picked his way through the scrub oak close to the wreck. He finally positioned the dozer on relatively firm earth, turned 180 degrees, and released the winch.

Pulling the steel cable, Toole sloshed through the mud to put a choker—a short cable with a loop at each end—around the differential and frame of the car, then hooked the cable to the choker. After returning to his rig, he carefully removed the slack from the cable, then slowly applied power. The cable tightened; the wrecked car shuddered as it went taut, and then yielded to the power of the dozer. After winching the car close to the dozer,

Ronnie moved forward onto dry ground, then slacked the cable, removed the choker, and rewound the cable on the winch. He attached the choker to the frame of the vehicle and fastened the other end to the hook at the top center of the dozer blade. He raised the blade forty-five degrees, lifting the car onto its side, then carefully reversed until the car rolled over onto its wheels.

The windshield frame and convertible top were crushed into the cockpit. Water dripped off a lifeless hand that hung from the partially opened door. Ray stepped forward and pulled on the door handle; the door was jammed. He tried the passenger door, it wouldn't open either.

Toole approached carrying a long, steel pry bar. "Let me get that open for ya, Sheriff."

"Go ahead, Ronnie."

Toole pushed the pry bar through the opening in the door, wedged it against the transmission tunnel, and threw his weight against it. The door gave slightly. Ray grabbed the opposite side of the bar and pulled as Ronnie pushed. With a grinding sound, the door grudgingly gave way. Ronnie extracted the bar. Ray dropped to his haunches and looked into car. He stood and said, "We've got to get the top off."

Toole pulled on the convertible top. "It's all busted, but it's still hooked together." He pulled a hunting knife from his belt, pointed it at the top, and looked at Ray. "Sheriff?"

"Go ahead," Ray responded.

Toole pushed the knife through the canvas near the front, half way across the top, and pulled the blade toward him. He made a small slash at right angles to the first, grabbed the flap of rotting canvas, and tore most of the convertible top from its crushed frame.

The body, soggy and mud covered, was pushed down and forward toward the firewall. Broken pieces of the steering wheel penetrated the chest, and the head hung to the side like a broken doll.

"Poor bastard didn't feel nutten. Probably dead as hell soon as he run off the road. Least he ain't rotten. I hate that stink." Toole lit a cigarette, inhaling deeply and exhaling through his nose and mouth. He asked, "Ya want me to pull it up to the road after they get the body."

"In a bit, we'll need some time to complete our investigation."

The EMTs had the body zipped in a bag and strapped in a wire basket when Deputy Sue Lawrence started down the embankment, camera in hand. Ray had watched her work her way down the hill, occasionally sliding on the wet grass and loose gravel.

"What kind of car is this?" she asked when she finally stood at his side.

"It's a Triumph, early 60s."

"And only one occupant?"

"Looks that way." He handed her a driver's license

"Roger Grimstock, Grand Rapids," Sue said looking at the license.

"He's a summer resident. He kept this car up here. I want photos of the car from all sides and from where it left the road to where it ended up over there." He pointed. "Let's see if we can reconstruct what happened."

As Sue photographed the wrecked car, the body was carried up the hill and loaded into an ambulance. She waded out into the swamp and positioned herself so she could capture the path made by the car on its way in, then they climbed back up to the highway.

"This is where the car left the road," said Ray, pointing to ruts obliquely cutting across the soft shoulder. They followed the trail the car had made through the brush and tall grass, Sue photographing where it had collided with trees as it careened and rolled down the steep embankment. Then they climbed back up the hill and walked along the road, carefully inspecting the pavement and the shoulder.

"There's a lot of oil here," Sue said, about fifty yards below where the car had left the road.

Ray knelt down and looked at the surface of the road. He pulled two fingers across the blacktop. He turned his hand over and smelled the grime on his fingertips. "Dirty engine oil." He walked to the edge of the road. "You can see where it ran on to the side here. See where it has soaked into the sand?"

"Does that mean something?" asked Sue.

"If it came from that car, maybe it threw a rod. If the engine seized, the rear wheels could have locked up."

"And?" said Sue with a questioning tone to her voice.

"And it might have caused the driver to lose control. One possibility. But then a variety of things might have happened. I just want to make sure there isn't anything to suggest that another car was involved. When we get the results of the post, we'll have another piece of the puzzle. Victim might have been drunk, or had a heart attack. We better see if we can find Grimstock's next of kin; the media will be hounding us for his name."

22

Ray found Marc sitting on the front deck, his feet on the rail, sipping a beer, Grendel sleeping at his side. The dog stood and barked at Ray's approach, but sprawled out again as soon as he recognized him.

"Want a beer?" Marc asked.

"Can't, I'm working. Just stopped by for a while. You looked like hell when you left the accident scene. I thought maybe it would help if I came by and talked with you about it."

"I guess it would help to talk. I don't know if I have worked it through enough yet. What about the car? "

"Well, it looks like the victim was dead soon after the car left the road. Probably broke his neck when the car went over. But it was good that you spotted the wreck."

"Who was it good for? Wasn't good for me; didn't matter to him."

"True, but the car could have stayed down there a long time without anyone ever seeing it. I don't think it would have ever been noticed by someone passing in a car or truck."

"And the victim?"

"Fellow by the name of Roger Grimstock. I knew the car as soon as I saw it. Summer resident. From Grand Rapids. Spent most of his time at the Last Chance. We occasionally would pick him up after closing when he couldn't keep his car on the road. I once found him drunk and asleep at the stop sign in Glen Arbor,:motor running, lights on, radio blaring, car sitting there idling away in neutral. Don't know what he was doing way over on Ely last night. I'm sorry you had to stumble on the wreck."

"I didn't need to find the car, but that doesn't have much to do with it. I woke up in the middle of the night in a cold sweat. I was in an absolute panic; I couldn't figure out what was causing it. Then it hit me that I may have made a big mistake."

"What kind of mistake? What are you talking about?" asked Ray.

"Moving here. It suddenly occurred to me that this has always been a place I stopped off at—a kind of never-never land that I visited when I was a kid. It was never a real place. My identity was always somewhere else. I also thought about the fact that I walked away from a career that took years to build; more than a career, an identity. I woke up wondering who I was now. Have I been too precipitous in making my decision?"

"Well," asked Ray, "is there any reason why you can't go back?"

"Well, no, but it would be embarrassing. I have always thought of myself as prudent and thoughtful in making big decisions. How would it look…"

"Relax. It's no big thing; people change their minds. Marc, your problem is you never allowed yourself to make a mistake. And if you made a mistake, you would live with it rather than admit it."

"What do you mean?" asked Marc.

"How about Elaine?" said Ray, showing some anger. "How many years did I have to come by and visit you with that cold bitch? I knew she didn't like me, but she didn't seem to like you very much either. I could tell this was a contract you had entered into, and you were bound and determined to make it work. You were always so fucking high-minded."

Marc let the comments about Elaine pass. He didn't want to talk about her. "You don't seem to understand. You don't hear what I'm saying. I have always defined myself with my work. My work has been central to my whole life. What would you be if you suddenly weren't the sheriff?"

"That's a real question, one I've thought about. It could happen. I like this work. It's interesting, and I have been involved in it a long time. But if it all stopped tomorrow I would be able to make the adjustment. I'm not saying I wouldn't miss being sheriff, but I could fill my time with other things that are worth doing. I could go back to college teaching; I could find work in industry. The thing that I would dislike most would be to have to move back to some urban area.

"Marc, I hate to give advice, but you're going to have to find some other things to do. You can only ride your bike and sail so many days. You're too 'type A' to be on a permanent vacation. I thought you might be having some romantic problems that I could help you with." Ray was giving Marc an ironic smile.

Marc didn't pick up on the humor. "Well, I'm worried about that too."

"What's wrong? She looks happy as hell. You must be doing all the right things," he said with a hint of lechery in his voice.

"Goddamn it, Ray, this is serious stuff. It is going well. That's what scares the hell out of me. It's going too well. I can't imagine that it will last."

"How long have you known her mother? Lisa's just a chip off the old block. You know what a good person Pat is, and she has never changed. Lisa has those same qualities. Your problem is you never had anyone be really good to you. I know your grandparents did all the right things for you—but they were a somber pair, so stiff and correct, there was never much joy around here. Pat was the first good thing that ever happened in your life. Her daughter is the second. Stop feeling guilty, her mother is delighted as hell knowing

you and her sweet daughter are having a wonderful time together—
new love is terrific. It's okay to stop and roll in the daisies. Enjoy
this lovely woman, enjoy living without analyzing everything, your
brain won't rot." Ray's voice turned serious, "You've always been
too damn rational. There are a hell of a lot of things in life that can't
be figured out logically. You need to take some time to understand
the feeling side of life. Just go with the feelings for a while. You can
figure it all out later. You're a good person, always have been. I've
been lucky to have you as a friend all these years."

"That was a hell of a sermon."

"Well, you needed a kick in the ass. What are friends for,
anyway? I've got to get back to work so you city folk don't continue
to kill yourselves off. I'll take a rain check on that beer. Maybe I can
stop back later tonight if things quiet down. I'll call you."

23

The driver killed the lights and turned off the pavement, pulling the rusting Pontiac far enough into the woods so it could not be seen from the road. The driver, and only occupant, dressed in a black T-shirt and jeans, opened the trunk, and unwrapped the AK-47 from an old cotton blanket. He walked through the woods to the west, his progress slowed by the heavy underbrush and the rapidly fading light. He found the sand road first, then moved along it until he could see the lights from the house. He stopped and slid a clip into the rifle.

When he got close enough, he could see there was only one car, a light-blue Mercury, parked at the side of the house. Then he saw headlights coming and moved to the side of the sand road, laying on his stomach in the thick underbrush. He heard the car stop, saw the lights go off. He waited. The car door opened, then closed. The driver, a tall male, was perfectly silhouetted against a large picture window as he walked toward the house.

Initially he fired two bursts separated by a second or two. Most of the bullets from the first burst hit the man, jolting him, tearing gaping holes as they exited. The second burst was high, exploded through the window, ripping through the plaster of the wall opposite the window.

The shooter liked the feeling the gun gave him. He liked the smell of the spent powder. He fired one more burst, blowing out the windows of the two parked cars.

24

It had been a late night for Ray. He and Sue had been at the scene of the shooting until well after 2:00 a.m. They had collected dozens of shell casings and found several clear prints left by the shooter's shoes. They made castings of the prints.

They had tried to question the victim's wife, but she was too hysterical. Ray thought her hysteria was a bit overdone, but decided not to pursue the questioning. He could accomplish more by waiting until morning.

The call from Reverend Tim came in just after Ray got to the office the next morning. The call had first been directed to Sue. She put the caller on hold and walked the few yards to Ray's open office door.

"Are you in and taking calls?" she asked.

"Who's asking?"

"It's a Reverend Tim; he doesn't seem to have a last name. He insists on talking to you. Do you want me to put him off?"

"I'll talk to him; might as well start the day with the bizarre."

"He's on three," said Sue.

Ray lifted the receiver and hit the blinking button. "Good morning, Reverend Tim."

"Good morning, Sheriff. Sheriff, you've got to come out and talk to me."

"I'd be happy to do that Reverend Tim, but I'm real busy with a murder investigation right now. Could I have one of the…"

"That's what I want to talk to you about, the Hammer murder. I know who done it. Can you come out here at once so I can tell you about it?"

"I'll come and see you, but can you give me some information on the phone?"

"Sheriff, the devil has got this phone tapped and he's telling the murderer everything. Please come and see me. I've got to unburden my heart of this."

"Reverend Tim, you can't come to the office, can you?"

"My truck ain't running. Will you come over?"

"I'll be there in twenty minutes to a half an hour. How does that sound?

"I'll be waiting, Sheriff."

Ray hung up the phone. He walked to Sue's desk.

"I'd like you to go with me on this one; bring a recorder and your laptop."

"Where are we going?"

"We're going to take a statement from Reverend Tim. You've never met him?"

"No, I've just heard stories."

Ray smiled. "This will be an interesting chapter in your education."

Ray drove out of the village, turned on Indian Hill Road, and headed north. After several miles he pulled onto Deadstream, a sand and gravel road that wound into a heavily wooded area. After a few miles Ray pointed out the sign—crudely hand lettered, white paint on a weathered board nailed to a tree—Freewill Bible Synod of God: the Only True Followers of Jesus. Below it was another sign. Its message, sprayed in phosphorescent orange, read, Jesus Loves Bikers.

Ray turned onto the two-track. The area was low and swampy until they reached a large clearing. A long, coarsely constructed church stood in the center and a cross made from two small logs lashed together with yellow nylon rope stood near the entrance. A pickup truck was parked under a large oak at the side of the church. The truck's engine was suspended from an overhead branch by a jerry-rigged system of ropes and pulleys.

At the right of the clearing stood a second building. The front of an old mobile home poked out of one end of a collection of tacked-on additions, giving the impression of a caterpillar covered by cancerous appendages.

Ray parked near the front door and the slamming of the car doors brought Reverend Tim rolling out of the church. Tim—clad only in large bib overalls, which he filled completely—wiped his hand on his hip and extended it to Ray. His hands and short, thick arms were covered with grease. He also had several streaks of grime across his face.

"Sheriff, glad ya come. I'd a been in to see you if this dang motor hadn't given up."

"We are happy to come to meet you. This," Ray motioned to Sue, "is Deputy Lawrence; she will be making notes of this conversation."

"Nice ta meet you, Miss," said Tim with a gesture that approached a bow, but not offering a hand. "Why don't we sit over there, Sheriff?" Tim led them to a small circle of benches—planks nailed to the tops of stumps.

Ray pushed ahead, "Reverend Tim, you said on the phone that you know who is responsible for the Hammer killing. We tried questioning Mrs. Hammer last night, but she was too upset to help us."

"No, wonder. That poor child." The words, although sympathetic in context, had a condemnatory tone. He paused and looked at Ray. "If she had stayed with Jesus, this would never have happened. She is a prisoner of Satan. She will tell you she loves Jesus, but I know who really owns her soul."

"Can you tell us what you know?" prodded Ray.

"I've knowed her since she was a child and there was always that wildness. You can see it in her eyes; she's possessed. There's always been a battle to keep the devil at bay, but I guess we've been losing it for a long while."

"You're talking about Kit Hammer?" asked Ray.

"Who do you think I'm talking about, Sheriff?" he responded crossly. "She's always been under his control. You don't know how many times I've prayed over that girl, but my power just isn't strong enough. The devil is able to creep into some folk. He's in their bones, he's in their muscles, he's in their brain, he's in their guts, he's even in their blood getting pushed around their body with every beat of their heart. You can do battle with Satan and almost defeat him, but he's just hiding in some corner. As soon as you're not watching, he comes rushing back. He takes the heart, takes the soul, and the rest is easy. He's had her since she was a little girl."

"Are you're saying that Mrs. Hammer is the murderer?" Ray asked.

"You're not listening, Sheriff. I didn't say that. What I said was that she is an agent of the devil. The devil worked through her to make this happen."

"I'm still not following; can you tell me who the killer is?"

"Well, I knowed it was going to happen. Last Sunday we was having a group confession and praying for the sinners. This one wasn't going too good; it takes a while for the folks to get it going, if you know what I mean. We get a lot of little sins confessed to until folks get worked into it a bit. Burt Watson confessed to selling a car with a bad engine, and the congregation prayed for Jesus to forgive him and that the engine might be healed so the buyer wouldn't suffer none. I hate it when stuff like that happens, like Jesus has nothing better to do then go around fixing old Chevrolets, but in this business you got to put up with that until folks get going and start talking about more interesting sins. Then Sarah Johnson tells the congregation about how her old man and her was poaching deers last winter. Everyone knows they need that meat to live, it ain't no big sin. I can tell people was getting pretty bored with this.

"Fortunately, Minnie Pfeiffer jumps up about then and starts speaking in tongues. This always gets everyone going cause they know the Holy Spirit is now in the room—most folks feel better about confessing their sins when they know for sure that someone is listening. Minnie, she goes on for a long while, and people were getting more and more excited to cast off their sins.

"About this time Kit Hammer comes to the front and starts screaming and yelling to Jesus to forgive her for her dreadful sin. I asked her to tell us about her sin, tell us which one of God's commandments she broke, but she won't for the longest time. I gets the congregation to chant 'Tell Mr. Jesus, tell Mr. Jesus' over and over until she says, 'I am guilty of adultery, please save my soul.' I wish you could have been there Sheriff. I wish you could have felt the presence of the Lord."

"I wish I had been," Ray offered. "Then what happened?"

"I asked her who she had sinned with so God would know who to punish." He stopped and looked at Ray, "God knows, but I wanted the brothers and sisters to know because God sometimes needs agents on earth to help do his work. She tells us it's Lennie Buck, and she tells us where he lives. And I could tell that we were ready to do God's work. I got the men; we piles into four or five trucks and drives to Buck's trailer—he only lives a couple miles from here. We busted the door, pulled that sinner out of his bed, dragged him out, and beat him real good. I wished we could have stoned him, but I know you just can't get by with that anymore. Then we came back here and thanked the Lord that he had let us do his work."

"How do you connect this to the death of Hammer?"

"When we went to punish this sinner, we held Buck while Hammer beat him up, not that he done it alone, most of us got a few good ones in. As we was leaving, Buck yells that he's gonna get even. I know what you're thinking, Sheriff—making threats doesn't mean anything—but Buck hollered that he was 'going to get a fucking machine gun and turn us all into hamburg.' That's what he said, and that's what he done."

Ray looked over at Sue who had been making notes during the conversation. "Do you have any questions for Reverend Tim?"

"About what time did this happen?"

"Service started about nine. It was probably ten thirty or eleven when Kit made her confession. I knowed we were back here by lunch time."

"Could you provide the names of others who could corroborate your story?"

"Well there was Jamie…" Reverend Tim went on to name eight men who accompanied him to Buck's trailer.

25

They were sitting on the deck facing the lake, a bottle of wine on the floor between them. Lisa, in one of Marc's chambray shirts, sleeves rolled up to the elbows, bare legs pulled up under her, held a wine glass mid-stem, and peered far out into the lake. Marc, shirtless, in faded khaki shorts, with bare feet pushed out in front of him, looked at her intensely as she spoke.

Ray came around the corner of the cottage, paused for a moment, and observed the scene. He felt uncomfortable interrupting.

"Well, while the rest of us have to work," he announced with a note of humor in his voice, climbing the steps onto the deck, "it looks like you are having a relaxing day."

They both jumped at the sound of his voice.

"Can I get you a glass of wine?" Marc asked, rising.

"Can't, on duty. We're about to make an arrest. Can't smell like wine when I talk to the press, can I?"

"An arrest at last! That's terrific; your arrest rate was starting to look like Detroit's," said Marc. "You nabbed a Mafia hit man?"

"Wrong murder. This is last night's murder off Indian Hill Road. Aren't you lovers aware of what is going in the world? Didn't you see me on the local news this morning?"

"Lisa's plane was delayed. It didn't get in until after midnight."

"Let's hear it, Chief," said Lisa playfully. "How did you solve it so quickly?"

"Well, I wish the other was like this," said Ray. "Last night about 10:30 we got a call about a shooting. Bob Kretchmer was in the area and got to the scene in a few minutes. The poor bastard had been ripped almost in two by a burst from an assault rifle. I got there ten or fifteen minutes later. At first the widow was hysterical and couldn't tell us anything. When she finally did settle down a bit, she was very uncooperative."

"Why?" asked Marc.

"Just wait, let me give you the story in sequence. There was a lot of evidence around. We found where the murderer parked; we got footprints, tire treads, couple dozen shell casings. Even without the murder weapon, loads of physical evidence. This morning I got a call from a local minister who said he knew who the killer was. He wouldn't tell me anything over the phone because he said Satan had his phone tapped. I went out and questioned him. He gave us the motive—motive of sorts—plus the name, address, the whole nine yards. I've got the suspect's place staked out; I'm on my way over there. State Police are coming to back us up with some heavy artillery in case the suspect decides to shoot his way out. "

"How did the minister know?" asked Lisa.

"I did use 'minister,' didn't I? Let me amend that. He calls himself Reverend Tim…"

"Reverend Tim—that sounds pretty down home?" interjected Lisa.

"Let me tell you," said Ray trying to affect a twang, "this here is a real preacher man. There is a little church on Deadstream Road—Freewill Bible Synod of God: the Only True Followers of Jesus—don't ask me where or how they got the name. It's a little log and slab-wood building way back off the road. You'd never find it if you didn't know exactly where it was. The stream runs behind the church, and they've dug it out and widened it so they can get the congregation in the water when they do baptisms."

"How do you know all this?" asked Marc.

"I had to investigate them a few years back. A summer kid from Birmingham got involved with the group and moved in with the minister and his family. The kid's family charged that he had been kidnapped by what they termed a 'satanic cult.' The family was well connected and we got put under a hell of a lot of pressure to find out about the church."

"So is it a satanic cult?" asked Lisa.

"No, but they spend a lot of time talking about Satan. They seem to believe that Satan and his henchmen are lurking behind every bush and tree. But it's really just a Bible thumping group Reverend Tim put together. Seems Mr. Jesus—that's the term Reverend Tim uses—talked to him one day when he was cutting wood and told him he was to start this church, even told him where to put it and how to build it."

"And he has a congregation?"

"Of sorts, about sixty or seventy people. Mostly old and poor, they live in shacks and old trailers in the area. It's a real flannel shirt and dirty jeans crowd."

"Don't expect they pull many from the summer set," Marc threw in sarcastically.

"Well, I don't think he pulls the yuppie crowd," responded Ray with a smile, "but they do get a few fudgies. In the summer they put out a big, hand-lettered sign by the road that reads, 'Jesus loves Bikers.' Some of the over-the-hill Harley crowd seem to worship there."

"The what?" asked Lisa.

"You've seen them. They probably took up biking after they saw Brando's film. They've got to be in their fifties or older, ride beat-to-shit Harleys with the leather fringes on their saddle bags dragging on the road. They all seem to have big guts and usually have women of about the same size riding behind them. I don't know how the bikes can take all that weight."

"And they go to this church?" asked Marc.

"In the summer they seem to be part of the congregation. But let me get back to my story. I had to check out this church—I even sat through services a number of times. Reverend Tim is quite mad, but he's good with words; his description of the wages of sin could rival Cotton Mather's. And when he really gets going, the congregation goes wild: people speak in tongues and yell and scream and beg for forgiveness. And his harangues last for hours…"

"And the kid from Birmingham?"

"Well, he was pretty freaky, too. But he was eighteen and he didn't seem to be held against his will—we questioned him carefully. His parents wanted us to physically remove him and have him deprogrammed. When we wouldn't, they were really pissed. But what the hell, they don't vote here, they just pay taxes."

"So what does this have to do with the murder?" asked Lisa.

"Well, Brother Tim called this morning. Seems the deceased and his wife were members of the congregation. During last Sunday's service they were having a special group confessional and praying for the sinners. This guy's wife, the wife of the now deceased, tells the congregation about how she's been seeing this other man. Reverend Tim gets her to tell all and after the service some of the men in the congregation, led by Tim and including her husband, go over to this guy's trailer and give him a good beating. As they were leaving he made lots of threats. So when Reverend Tim heard Joe Hammer got murdered, he called and asked me to come out so he could tell me about what had happened."

"The guy's name is Hammer. Any relation to…"

"You got it, Lisa. First cousin."

"Unbelievable," said Lisa. "And the rest of the story—is the murderer a local?"

"No, he's an unemployed auto worker—got laid off from a plant in Pontiac and moved up here. He's been a suspect in some cottage break-ins, but we've never been able to nail him."

"Are you going to have trouble arresting him?" asked Marc.

"I don't know. If he's really in his trailer, he's in an impossible situation. Watch the news."

26

The staging area for the assault on Lennie Buck's trailer was at an old cemetery about a mile down the road. Ray stood in the center of the small circle of his deputies and State Police Troopers.

"First, I don't want any of you wounded or killed. We will take our time; we have all of the advantages. The trailer is in the open and you can drive off the road to take your positions. Stay behind your cars because there is no other cover.

"Second, I want to take Buck prisoner. If possible, I don't want him injured. We know he has an AK-47. We don't know how much ammunition. So please be careful.

"Once we are all in place I'll try to talk him out with a bull horn. If that doesn't work, we'll try some tear gas. Again, be careful. This man has nothing to lose. He's very dangerous."

The old trailer stood in the middle of a flat, sandy field. An old Pontiac was parked near the front door. One by one the police cars rolled off the road and formed a distant circle around the trailer. The police got out and took cover. Ray was the last in line and positioned his car across from the trailer's entrance.

He stood, the car door ajar, looking over the hood at the trailer. He lifted the bullhorn.

"Lennie Buck, we know you're in there. We have the place completely surrounded—there's no escape. I want you to open the door wide and come out slowly with both hands high in the air. And I want you to keep those hands high." Ray tried to think about what might be going through Lennie's head as a way of thinking about what he should prepare for. A vision of Jackson Prison flashed before Ray. If he were in Lennie's shoes, he would rather die than go to Jackson.

The instant Ray heard the glass break he dropped behind his car. A short blast from the assault rifle raked his car and sent puffs of sand flying on the surrounding ground.

"Are you all right, Ray?" someone asked on the radio.

"Yes. Put in some tear gas."

Ray heard the shot and then heard, "Shit, I missed the window. I'll fire a second one." The second shot sounded, and then, "That one's in and smoking."

"Nothing happening," came another voice.

"Put in another one," said Ray.

He heard the third shot. He looked over his hood and watched the smoke roll out of the windows."

"There's a fire," came a voice.

Ray saw the flames pushing out of the front window of the trailer. The door of the trailer opened a crack and stopped. The deputies tensed, ready to fire. Then the door slowly opened the rest of the way. A man emerged, staggered a few feet, and fell to his hands and knees. The fire quickly engulfed the whole trailer; the man crawled forward, away from the heat. Ray approached him from one side, Bob Kretchmer approached from the other side, pulling a pair of handcuffs from a case on his belt and securing Lennie's arms behind his back.

The man was limp. Ray pulled Lennie to his feet and dragged him away from the burning trailer, back behind his car. The fire roared through the flimsy structure, burning through the aluminum skin on the roof. Ammunition exploded in the flames.

Buck, in dirty jeans and a black T-shirt with Shit Happens in block letters on the front, slouched against the side of Ray's car. His head was down as if he were examining his shoeless feet. His figure, long and lean with round shoulders suspended on a narrow frame, hung with a look of defeat. A thin nose separated two small, watery blue eyes. A long, shaggy beard framed the pale-white face.

Ray read Buck his rights; the prisoner nodded as if he understood, but said nothing. Ray motioned to Bob Kretchmer. "Get him out of here."

Ray walked back toward the trailer. The roof had collapsed, and as he watched, the wall near him peeled away like someone doing a back dive in slow motion. The wall on the other side of the trailer soon followed in the opposite direction. By the time the volunteer fire department arrived, there was little to do but dampen the remains and put out a few small grass fires near the ruins.

Ray circled the trailer with Sue looking at the rubble. Finally he said, "There it is," and pointed at a metal object entangled in springs and half-burned wood that once formed a day bed. He borrowed some heavy leather gloves from the fire crew and carefully fished the remains of the AK-47 out of the smoldering mass.

"Not bad," said Ray.

Sue gave him a quizzical look.

"We've got motive, foot prints, tire prints, and the weapon, albeit slightly charred. If we get a confession, it will be as clean as it can be. It's nice getting one solved quickly for a change."

27

Through the open window, Jack Grochoski saw the Sheriff's car pull up to the side of the bar. By the time Ray walked into the Last Chance, Jack had two cups on the bar and was filling them with coffee.

"Good timing, Sheriff; this is a fresh pot."

"Thanks, Jack." Ray took a sip. "Jack, you make about the best coffee in the county."

"It's the water, Sheriff, it's the water. I don't use well water. I get spring water in those big bottles; well water has too much iron, makes the coffee bitter. Don't imagine you came by to talk about coffee."

"Grimstock, Roger Grimstock, was he in here on Saturday evening?"

"Thought you'd be by to ask 'bout him. He was here. Has been almost every summer night for years. You probably know that."

Ray nodded, "I wasn't sure about Saturday night, but I did know his car was usually in your lot. Anything different about Saturday night? Was he drinking heavily?"

"He was the same as always. I imagine he started drinking when he got out of bed. He'd come in here in the early evening and have a couple shots-and-beers, and then he'd settle down to just beers, Budweiser in bottles. He'd drink about one an hour until he left, usually 'bout closing, sometimes before. He was never falling down drunk; he always seemed in control—you know I cut people off it they're not. But he was never stone sober, probably hadn't been in years."

"Did he have any friends, anyone he met here?"

"He was a real fixture here, but I don't think anyone knew him; I sure didn't. Over the years I watched people try to get a conversation going with him, but he'd cut them off. He wanted to be left alone. The girls that work here were all afraid of him because he'd snap at them. Had a nasty mouth."

"And Saturday was just the same?"

"Well, I have to be truthful. He was like an old piece of furniture—you might walk by it ten times a day and you don't notice it. I know he was here; I remember serving him; I remember he was on his usual stool, and he wasn't here at closing. But there was one peculiar thing."

"What's that?"

"He got a phone call sometime late in the evening. Years ago, when he was still married, his wife would call here all the time looking for him, but I don't think he's had a call since they split up."

"Man or woman—the person on the phone?"

"Man or woman," Jack repeated. "That's interesting, Sheriff. I don't remember. It gets real noisy here at night and my hearing ain't what it was. I might guess that it was a woman, but that's probably because the only calls we get here are women looking for their men. I don't think I can say for sure."

"So he got this call late in the evening. What time would that be?"

"It probably was between eleven and twelve. The summer crowd doesn't start dropping off until after midnight."

"Did he leave right after he got the call?"

"I can't say, Sheriff. I don't think so. I just know he was gone before closing."

"Is that unusual?"

"Most nights he's here till then, but sometimes he leaves around midnight, sometimes before. Usually buys a six pack on his way out."

"Jack, is there anything else you can remember about Saturday?"

"I don't think so. I've pretty much told you all I know."

"If you think of anything, please give me a call. It gives me an excuse to get some more of this good coffee."

28

~~~~

Dell's Complete Auto Service was housed in two buildings. The first, the smaller of the two, looked like a 50s gas station. In the middle 80s the interior walls were removed so the business could function as both a convenience store and gas station. The service part of the business was moved to a large pole building behind the first.

Ray found Dell working on a truck engine, its cab tipped forward to allow access to its innards.

"Looks like you could get lost in there," said Ray as a way of getting Dell's attention.

Dell, hearing the comment, turned and looked at Ray. Dell—well into his seventies, with heavily muscled biceps extending from a short sleeved shirt, his stomach hanging over his belt—climbed down from the truck. He pushed his glasses back up to the bridge of his nose with a grease-covered hand. "I wish the bastards that designed these things would have to try to fix them. There's only a little problem with that damn truck, but you have to spend half the day getting to it. And Bill VanDyke will bitch like hell when he finds that I've charged him four hours labor to replace a ten dollar part."

"Why don't you charge him more for the part and less for labor? Use a little psychology on him."

"Won't work on that damn old Dutchman, Sheriff. He checked on how much the part cost before I started the job."

"Dell, that old Triumph they brought in from the accident scene. Did you have a chance to check it over?"

"I went through it. It's back in the storage area."

"How about the brakes and steering?

"Brakes was okay, and there was nothing wrong with the steering. Let me show you, it's over here." Dell led Ray to a fenced area behind the building.

"As you know, everything is pretty banged up and bent, but nothing is broken in the steering. Tie rods are still intact and the rack seems to be working all right. Look." Dell reached in, grabbed the wheel and moved it back and forth. He pointed to the front wheels, "See, there's some slop in it, but it works. Now the back wheels, that's another story."

"What do you mean?"

"Actually, Sheriff, it's not the rear wheels, it's the whole damn drive train. The whole thing is locked up."

"Why's that?"

"The motor came apart. I got the oil pan over here. I pulled it to look at the bottom of the engine. There are a couple of holes that were made when the engine came apart. The crank busted in half; the pan was full of metal debris."

"Any reason for that to happen?"

"It's an old engine. Looks like he was driving it wide open. You just can't do that with one of these. Probably was low on oil. Hard to tell what failed first, but what ever it was, the whole damn thing came apart instantly. The way things are jammed in here, it locks up the rear wheels."

"That explains a couple of things."

"Like?"

"We found oil on the road. And if the rear wheels locked up, he probably went into a skid and lost control of the car. Did you find anything else interesting?"

"One more thing." He pointed into the engine bay. The hood was missing from the car.

"What am I looking at?"

"These are old Stromberg 175s carburetors, a peculiar bit of limey engineering. Fucking limeys. You could never get these damn things synchronized."

"So, what about them?"

"Look, Sheriff, they're jammed wide open. The linkage is bent here and doesn't move. I don't know if this happened before the crash. It might have caused the accident. Or it might have happened in the course of the car rolling down the hill and smashing into things."

"Is there any chance that another vehicle was involved in the accident?"

"I don't think so. Every damn panel on this piece of shit is smashed, but I think that it happened when the car rolled down that hill. I don't see no paint on this other than dark green. That poor bastard picked about the steepest hill in the county for his accident. There's one more thing, the frame is busted in the back. It must've been almost rusted through."

"Could that have happened before the accident?"

"I don't think so, Sheriff. See where the rear quarter is smashed in here," Dell knelt beside the back of the car and ran his hands over the area. "The car must have hit a tree and most of the blow was carried by the wheel and axle. You can see bark and wood ground into these holes in the wheel. The axle being pushed sideways is what busted the frame, but it had to be weak to start with. I can have the boys put the car on the rack if you want to see where the frame is busted."

"No, Dell, I trust your judgment. You know much more about these things than I do."

"Sheriff, how long do you want me to keep this around?"

"It will probably take three or four weeks to get the whole thing cleared up. Don't do anything until you hear from us, and don't let me forget that it's here."

"I wouldn't do that Sheriff," Dell said with a big grin. "I wouldn't want to burden the tax payers with an unnecessary storage fee."

29

Ray was sitting at the oak table in the interrogation room. Sue was sitting at his right with a tape recorder and a laptop computer. Lennie was ushered in and seated across from Ray. His lawyer, Ilene Hawthorne, a court appointed attorney, seated herself at Lennie's right and opened her brief case, removing a yellow legal pad and a pencil. She was carrying extra weight from a recent pregnancy and filled her business suit. Her hair style, short and curled, did little to offset her coarse facial features: lips too large and full for her small face; a large flat nose with upturned, oval nostrils; a wide, tall forehead that sloped back to the curls; and eyes, small and angry, their size contrasting sharply with the grossness of her other features. She opened her purse and pulled a pair of glasses from a case. She lifted them to her face and carefully adjusted them. She did everything very slowly, knowing that all the attention was on her. "Sheriff, was my client adequately Mirandized?" she asked in an accusatorial tone.

"Yes, Ms. Hawthorne. It was the first thing we did after we took him into custody. If you check with your client, I'm sure he will remember my reading him his rights and asking if he understood what had been read to him."

"I asked him; he seemed confused, but given the excessive force used to make this arrest, it's no wonder."

Ray could feel his pulse throbbing against his collar; he imagined that his face was growing red. He tried not to respond too quickly, taking several breaths, concentrating on inhaling slowly, holding the air for several seconds, then slowly exhaling. When he felt in control he said, "The force used at the scene of the arrest was appropriate given the weapon the suspect was thought to have in his possession. In point of fact, the suspect did have an assault rifle and did use it when we attempted to arrest him. We used three canisters of tear gas. No bullets were fired by any police officer. We have the AK-47 Mr. Buck fired at us, lots of spent cartridges, and four bullet holes in the side of my car. There are a score of witnesses to his use of this weapon, including members of my department and the state police." Ray could hear the tension in his voice.

"And you all sing the same party line when anyone suggests that you used excessive force. I think the public is on to your little game," she responded with a sarcastic chuckle.

Ray let her comment pass and turned his attention to Lennie Buck. "Did you know Kit Hammer?"

"I have instructed my client to answer no questions until we go to trial, Sheriff."

"Ms. Hawthorne, you can instruct your client to do or not to do anything you want. But I have the authority and right under our system to question Mr. Buck. Mr. Buck, being competent, can decide whether or not he is going to answer my questions. You don't get to speak for him."

"I won't have my client badgered or intimidated."

Again Ray didn't respond to her comment. "Let me repeat the question for you again, Lennie. Did you know Kit Hammer?"

"That's a dumb question, Sheriff. By now everyone knows that."

"I told you not to answer any questions," commanded Hawthorne.

"Lady, I didn't ask for you. Stay the fuck out of my face. I'll say what I want to say, and you can go to hell."

"You do what I tell you. Do you want to spend the rest of your life in Jackson?"

"Like I care," he responded.

"Sheriff," Hawthorne began, "I need to talk with my client alone for a few minutes. I'm not sure we are communicating effectively with one another."

Ray was struck by the fact that her tone was almost pleasant. He got up; Sue followed his lead. "When you're ready, let the deputy know and we'll try again."

As they left Ray pulled the door closed and had a word with the deputy posted outside. "Let's get some air," he said to Sue. They exited out the back door and sat on a sandbank above the parking lot.

"It's times like this that I really miss cigarettes. When you're angry or tense, that's when a cigarette is wonderful."

"I don't know how you kept your cool; she's really vicious," said Sue.

"I've had to deal with her a number of times in the last several years. I think I'm starting to get used to her style. Her pregnancy was rumored to be very difficult. I enjoyed not having to deal with her the last six or eight months."

"How does someone as nasty as that get pregnant?" she asked.

"I suspect the usual way. I can't imagine that she would do anything immoral or unnatural."

Sue slapped at his arm with the back of her hand. "You men are all alike. What I'm saying is how could someone sleep with such an unpleasant person?"

"Maybe she is sweet and loving at home. Perhaps she reserves her ugly side for public occasions…"

"Sheriff, they're ready," came a summons from the deputy at the back door.

They reentered the interview room and took the same chairs they had previously occupied.

"Lennie, I was trying to establish that you knew Kit Hammer."

"Yes, I knew her."

"Remember my instructions," urged Hawthorne.

"I say what I want, and you can go to hell, lady."

Hawthorne jumped to her feet and shouted, "I am not going to sit through this. I'm not going to watch this judicial travesty."

"Ms. Hawthorne," said Ray in a calm voice, "it's important that you stay. We want to make sure Mr. Buck's constitutional rights are not abridged in any way."

Regaining control, she settled back into her chair.

"This is what happened Sheriff: I started seeing Kit in November or December, not too long after I moved up here. I was at the laundromat in Thompsonville doing my wash, and Kit was there. We talked while we waited and she helped me fold my clothes. I usually don't fold them, just throw 'em in a bag. We were the only ones there most of the time. She told me she was having lots of marital trouble. Her husband was some kind of religious nut that made her go to this real strict church. She wanted to know where I lived, and I told her.

"A couple of days later she shows up at my trailer with a bottle of whiskey and some beers. She tells me she's lonely. We get sorta smashed, and she just starts taking off her clothes and tells me she needs to be fucked. She was really a hungry bitch. She told me her husband hadn't been fucking her as some sort of punishment.

"At first I didn't care about her none, but hell, it was a free piece of ass a couple of times a week. Then I really started liking her.

"Somehow her husband found out she was messing around. He beat the hell out of her until she told him everything. He said if she ever seen me again he'd kill both of us. She snuck back and told me.

"Somehow he found out about that, too, and beat the hell out of her again. He told her that he'd kill me if she didn't confess to her sins in front of the whole fucking congregation at that church they go to.

"She did, and those bastards came over to my place. I was still sleeping. They busted in, dragged me outside, and messed me up pretty good. That was Sunday. Monday, after her old man goes to work, she comes over and says that I got to do something. She says he's going to kill me and probably kill her, too. She asks me if I'm going to run. I tell her I don't have enough gas to get to TC, and I don't have no money. How am I going to run? She gives me this big roll of bills she says she's been saving for a long time. She says I got to do something. Then she fucks me real good and tells me this is what it could be like every day if she could get away from her old man."

"Lennie, did she ever say to you directly that she wanted you to kill her husband?" Ray waited for Hawthorne to object, but she just sat silently and glared at him.

"Not that way, but I knew what she was getting at."

"Then what happened?"

"I took the money, went to that gun shop at Cedar Junction. They had a big display of those AK-47s with a sign that said you should buy one before the law changed. I had enough for one of them and a bunch of ammo."

"Did the clerk question you why you wanted that particular type of weapon?"

"No, but he seemed happy as hell that I was buying it. He said the pointy heads in Congress was trying to outlaw them and peace loving citizens should have the right to defend themselves."

"Did he have you fill out the gun purchase forms?"

"He had the forms, but he filled them out. He was a bit bothered that my driver's license didn't match my current address, but he said that nobody would notice, and it really didn't matter.

"I took the gun home and practiced a bit. I've never been much of a shot, but with one of those it doesn't matter much. You just aim, and it throws out a shit load of bullets."

"Tell me about the night of the shooting," said Ray.

"I knew from what Kit told me that Joe worked till nine in the summer. At first I thought I'd get him when he left the store, but I was afraid there'd be too many people around, so I decided to get him when he came home.

"I left my car by the highway and got a hiding place near their house. When he came home from work, I waited until he got out of his car, and blew the hell out of him."

"Then what did you do?"

"I stopped and had a couple of beers and a pizza at the Village Tap. Then I got a bottle and went home and drank until I passed out. I didn't hear nothing until you was shouting for me to come out."

"Lennie, why didn't you take off? You must have known that we would find you fairly quickly if you went back to your trailer."

"Where was I gonna run to? I got no money, I got no place to go. I've been to Jackson before, probably you know that. I'm not afraid to go back."

"But this time you're going for life," said Ray.

"We'll see about that," said Hawthorne. "There's not much of this that will be admissible."

Lennie continued, "Being out ain't much better than being in. At least there you know what tomorrow will bring."

Ray went to the door and got the deputy. He turned to Hawthorne, "If you don't have further need of your client, I'll have him returned to his cell."

"Not now," she responded.

After he was escorted from the room, Hawthorne said, "You won't get to use any of this."

"Counselor, I'm sure that you and the judge and prosecutor will have an interesting time working out what's admissible and what isn't."

She glared at him as she gathered up her things. She slammed the door behind her.

They sat there for a few minutes in silence. "It's interesting," began Sue, "the only time Buck showed any emotion was when he was pushing back against Hawthorne. I don't think I've ever seen someone so completely defeated, so hopeless. I'm surprised he cared enough for Kit, or was he angry enough to kill Hammer?"

"Which was it?" asked Ray. "Did he do it for love or was he just trying to get revenge for the beating?"

"I don't know. There was so little affect. I think he cares about her, or at least appreciates the fact that she cared about him."

"And does she care about him? What's your best guess based on what he's said?"

"Hard to tell. She might care, or she might have been just using him for sex or companionship."

"Does he know the difference between right and wrong?"

"Hard to tell," said Sue. "What do you think?"

"I think he knows; I don't think that there is any question about that. But he doesn't care. I don't think he sees any of his actions or their consequences as having real meaning, any importance."

"It would be much easier if people were either good or evil. It's never that neat, is it?"

"Never."

30

The lot was empty except for a pickup that, by the markings on the side, obviously belonged to the owner. Bud had converted a general store to his gun shop when he moved up from downstate in the early seventies. He had had the clapboard siding covered with rough-cut cedar to give the building a more rustic appearance. Next to the front door, with red, white, and blue ribbon streamers hanging on the side, was a sign that read AK-47 Freedom Sale Now In Progress. Ray noted at the bottom of the sign a bumper sticker with "Fire the Wimp, Hire a Hammer."

Ray pushed his way through the heavy front door. The high tin ceilings, installed when the building was constructed in the early days of the century, remained. The walls were covered with the heads of deer. A stuffed grizzly lunged from one side of the store, its mouth open, its arms and long claws reaching into the room. A moose, sad and mangy, peered from the back of the store toward the freedom of the parking lot. Smaller animals—a fox, a wolf, a badger, a porcupine, a wild turkey, a pair of wood ducks, and pheasant—stood on wooden shelves and stared through lifeless glass eyes.

Bud, in his late sixties, was standing behind a glass showcase at the back of the store. He was wearing khaki pants and a shirt with a military-style web belt and brass buckle. A string tie hung on his chest: a Petoskey stone cut in the shape of the Michigan mitten was centered on the two strands of the tie.

Bud, his arms in front of him, his large hands on the counter, fingers spread, rocked his large frame forward. "Good morning, Sheriff."

"Good morning, Bud."

"Something I can help you with, Sheriff?"

"We are investigating the Hammer murder. We found an AK-47 at the scene of the arrest, and the suspect, Lennie Buck, said he bought the weapon here on Monday. I want to confirm that this information is correct."

"That's correct, Sheriff. Although I'll have to check on the day, but I'm pretty sure it was Monday. We've had a lot of action on those AK-47s. Surprised you haven't been in to pick up a few for the department. With all the riffraff coming up from downstate, I'd sure want my people to have adequate fire power to protect themselves." Bud gave him a sardonic grin.

Ray let the comment pass. "Would you please show me the paper work on the sale?"

"I've got it all right here, Sheriff. As you know we do everything by the book." Bud turned to a tall, gray file cabinet and rifled through the top drawer, and then the second drawer. Finally, he extracted a worn manila folder, smudged and tatty, from the drawer. "His application is right here, Sheriff," he said laying a slightly rumpled sheet on the glass-topped counter.

Ray looked at the application. "Did he fill this out himself?"

"No, I helped, but all the information came from him. He seemed to have trouble reading the form, so, in the interest of accuracy, I read it to him and copied his responses; it's just the same as if he did it himself. And that is his signature at the bottom. He signed it himself."

Ray studied the form carefully. "Bud, it says here that Mr. Buck is a resident of this county and lives at an address on Indian Hill Road. His driver's license has him living in Flint, in Genessee County."

"Yes, Sheriff, he told me he had moved and was going to get that corrected right away. I thought it was better to record his current address, just to get things right. You know how slow bureaucracies are. That's not going to cause any trouble, is it?"

Ray didn't respond; he just kept perusing the form as if he hadn't heard the question. After several minutes he asked, "Did you wait on Mr. Buck?"

"I'm the only one here, Sheriff, except during deer season when my brother-in-law comes in to help."

"What can you tell me about Mr. Buck?"

"He was waiting in the parking lot when I got here; I guess it was sometime after nine. He said he wanted a deer rifle."

"And you showed him a deer rifle?"

"I started to, one of the new Winchesters that's real popular, but then he said he wanted to see an AK-47."

"Did that strike you as strange?"

"I'm never surprised by what some of those fudgies come up with; besides, the liberal media has given these weapons such a bad rap, lots of honest folks are embarrassed to ask for one. And I told that young man that if he wanted one of these," he turned and picked one off the rack behind him, "he'd better buy one while he still could. Ain't that right, Sheriff?"

"How much ammunition did Mr. Buck purchase?"

"He purchased two hundred rounds."

"Isn't that an unusually large quantity?"

"It's a lot, but these guns use a lot. You can go through that much in a few minutes of target shooting. Besides, I urge people to buy a lot just in case the government tries to ban the sale of ammo for this type of gun."

"Can you tell me about how he acted?"

"He just acted normal. As I was telling you, he said he wanted a deer rifle; then he got interested in this baby. These are fun, Sheriff. You should try one." He handed the rifle across the counter; Ray made no effort to take it, and he pulled it back. "Buck just seemed like a normal kind of person. Nothing really strange, I mean long hair used to bother me, but now it's just common. He seemed normal, you know what I mean? I was surprised to hear about the shooting. But, Sheriff, you need to know that the gun had nothing do with the killing. If he was determined to kill Joe Hammer, he would have found a way. He could have run him over, or used an axe, or knife, or even a broken beer bottle. People kill people, guns don't. But I will tell you one thing."

"What's that Bud?"

"He didn't really seem like a sportsman. You can usually tell. He was too much of a fudgie. Joe Hammer, on the other hand, he was a real sportsman and one hell of a shot. He killed damn near everything that moved. He was a good customer, too. I'll miss him."

Bud thrust the AK-47 in Ray's direction again. "Sure you don't want to get some of these? I'll give your department a hell of discount."

"Thanks for the help, Bud," said Ray as he headed for the door.

31

Ray's first trip to Joe Hammer's was the night of the shooting. In the darkness he was able to notice little of the exterior. His second trip was made in the brilliant light of a summer morn. Sue accompanied him. The house was long and low and centered in a clearing of scrub oak. The exterior was covered with a variety of materials, most of which looked like they had been scavenged from abandoned buildings. The rusting hulks of two derelict cars and one pickup were off to the side, next to a partially collapsed shed. In front of the house were the two bullet-riddled cars; most of their windows shattered. The picture window in the front of the house was covered with plastic sheeting held in place by thin pieces of wood tacked to the frame.

Two small children were playing in the sand next to the house. When Ray and Sue got out of the car, the children ran to a screen door. Ray and Sue followed.

Kit Hammer was standing at the door. "Can I help you, Sheriff?"

"Mrs. Hammer, we have got some questions we would like you to help us with."

"I told the deputy all I knew the other night."

"We need to go over a few things again and ask you some additional questions. May we come in?"

"I wasn't expecting no company, and the place is a mess. But," she completed the sentence with a tone of resignation in her voice, "come on in. You can sit at the table if you like. Let me clear a few things."

She rushed in front of them and removed several bowls with the remains of cereal and milk. Then she wiped the table and motioned them to sit. "Would you like coffee, Sheriff and Miss…"

"This is Sue Lawrence; she is helping with the investigation. I'd love some coffee, how about you?"

"Yes, please," said Sue.

Kit picked three cups from a pile of dirty dishes in the sink, rinsed them, and set them, still wet, on the table. Then she brought a battered aluminum coffeepot from the stove and filled the cups with a dark, thick liquid.

"Do you want anything in your coffee?"

They both gave a negative nod.

The two children stood quietly, watching the activity. "You kids go out and play," Kit ordered. They disappeared out the screen door. Another child appeared; a tall, frail girl of eleven or twelve. "Melody, go look after the kids while I talk to the Sheriff." The girl headed in the direction of her siblings.

"She was real close to her stepfather," said Kit. "She's hardly said anything the last several days."

"Mrs. Hammer, we don't want to take much of your time. We just have a few routine questions that we need to ask to get this thing cleared up. Then we won't have to bother you any more. How long were you and Mr. Hammer married?"

"We got married five years ago. The youngest boy, Junior, that's Joe's."

"Then you were married before?"

"No, Joe was my first husband. I had Melody when I was in high school, but I stayed with my parents. Later, when I had Billy, I was living with another man. We always said we'd get married, but he turned out to be real mean. I was living back with my parents when I met Joe. I got hired during the summer at the IGA where Joe was a butcher."

"You and Mr. Hammer, did you get along?"

"At first we were real happy. Joe was the first man that was good to me. But about two years ago he got involved with the Freewill Bible Church, you know about that?"

"Yes."

"Well, things went bad after Joe joined that church. He got real religious. From that time he wasn't no fun anymore, and he was always after me to change. He stopped smoking and drinking, wouldn't take me dancing. And the worst thing was that he made me go to church with him. Sometimes we'd spend all Sunday at that stupid church. And then the beatings started."

"Beatings?"

"I wouldn't stop smoking and drinking. So Brother Tim told him it was a husband's right to demand that his wife love him and honor his rule, and if she didn't, he had the right to use the rod until she obeyed."

"How often did this happen?"

"At first it was only occasionally, and I thought it would pass, but then Brother Tim told him that God was demanding that I stop sinning and he had to beat me to save my soul."

"When did you meet Lennie Buck?"

"It was last fall or winter. I met Lennie at the laundromat. He was lonely, and nice, and would listen. Joe stopped listening to me years ago. He just talked at me. Lennie and me, we kinda got involved. I don't know how Joe found out. I guess someone saw my car at Lennie's trailer and told Joe about it. One day he takes me out in the woods away from the kids and tells me he knows all about it, and then he starts beating me. He makes me tell him everything, then he makes me go through everything and starts beating me again when I stop. It was like he was getting some weird pleasure out of making me tell him. He tells me that Brother Tim says that I should be stoned to death, that's what the Bible says is

the punishment for adultery. He tells me that he'll spare my life
for the sake of the kids if I beg for Jesus's forgiveness at church on
Sunday."

"And you did," said Ray. "We've heard you did."

"But what I didn't know was that it was all planned. It was
planned for the men in the congregation to go over and beat up
Lennie. I guess that Joe was the worst of all. He used an axe handle
on him. Joe told me if I ever saw Lennie again he would kill both
of us. But I didn't care. As soon as Joe went to work I went over
to see if Lennie was all right. He told me he was going to kill the
bastard, but I told him not to do it. I thought he was just mad, that
he would get over it. The next night when Joe got home, Lennie
killed him. As soon as I heard the shots I knew it was Lennie."

"And," said Ray, "you didn't say anything to Lennie when you
saw him that might make him think you wanted him to kill your
husband?"

"No. I probably agreed with him that it would be nice if Joe
was gone. Then I would be rid of him. But I didn't tell him to kill
Joe."

"Did you give Lennie some money?"

"Yeah."

"Why did you give him money?"

"He didn't have none."

"The money, what was he suppose to do with it?"

"I told you. He didn't have none. He needed to get away. Joe
wasn't done with him."

"Did Joe tell you that?"

"No, but I know Joe. He'd find a way to get Lennie."

"How much money did you give Lennie?"

"Couple hundred, maybe three. Didn't really count it. I'd
been saving a little back for more than a year. Money I might use
to leave Joe.

"What am I going to do now, Sheriff? I got three kids and no
husband to support us. What am I going to do now?" She looked
across the table at him.

"Deputy Lawrence will arrange to have the people from social services meet with you. They should be able to provide you with some help. But it will be difficult." Ray stood, "I'm probably going to need to ask you some more questions in the next few days. Stay in the area."

"Where can I go Sheriff?" she asked as she walked them to the door. As Ray pushed the screen door open, the three kids came darting past them into the house.

They did not talk until Ray pulled back onto the highway. "What do you think?"

Sue shook her head. "I don't know, Ray. I just don't know."

32

John Tyrrell's tenure as Cedar County prosecutor started twenty years before Ray was elected to his first term. Tyrrell was only a few years out of law school when he was elected the first time. He had aspired to a judgeship a time or two during his career as prosecutor, but the voters were reluctant to endorse him. Although he was very popular and influential in local politics, his reputation as a bit of a drunk and a womanizer must have suggested to them that his expertise was more appropriately applied as a prosecutor than as a judge.

Early in Ray's tenure, the state police had arrested Tyrrell for DUI. Tyrrell had asked Ray to "cut a deal" with the state police and get the ticket torn up. Ray's refusal had set the tone for a relationship that was, although not rancorous, never truly cordial.

Tyrrell sat behind a massive walnut desk, a copy of the county seal on the wall behind him. Now well into his fifties, Tyrrell had run to fat. His head was unusually round and its shape was accentuated by his completely-bald head. His eyes bulged from his face.

Although the Cedar County Center had been a smoke-free building for more than a year, when Ray entered Tyrrell's office the

stench of cigar smoke was almost overwhelming. In the few months
since Ray had given up smoking, he had grown to dislike the smell
of cigarettes and cigars and had become increasing intolerant of
smokers.

"What do you have for me, Ray?"

"I think that the Hammer murder is pretty clean. You can
get Buck for murder one. We have lots of physical evidence, the
weapon, and paper work from Bud's showing that Buck bought
it the day before the murder. We have a statement from Reverend
Tim and several of his congregation that Buck threatened
Hammer. We have a statement from Hammer's wife. And last, we
have Buck's statement admitting to the crime; although I'm sure
Ms. Hawthorne will try her best to keep the statement from being
admitted as evidence."

"That woman's a real bitch. I was hoping she would never
come back from maternity leave. Is there any reason to think that
she might get away with it?"

"Not with Judge Murphy. You know we are very careful
about upholding Miranda. We read Buck his rights at the time of
the arrest. We didn't question him until the court had appointed
counsel. We asked questions and he answered them, answered
them over her objections."

"What if she goes for change of venue?"

"I don't think she'll get it. But even if she does, I don't think
there are weaknesses in procedures or the evidence."

"I'm glad you've wrapped this one up so quickly. I like
murder trials. The Holden case made me afraid I'd have to do a
guest appearance on Unsolved Mysteries." Tyrrell smiled at Ray,
which meant he opened a long slit of a mouth to show two rows
of yellow teeth.

"There's another matter involving this case that you'll have to
make a determination on."

"What's that?" asked Tyrrell.

"Joe Hammer's wife, Kit. Lennie Buck said that she told him to kill her husband. Let me read you that part of the statement." Ray leafed through the typed statement.

"'That was Sunday. Monday, after her old man had gone to work, she comes over and says that I got to do something. She says that he's going to kill me and probably going to kill her, too. She asks me if I'm going to run. I tell her I don't have enough gas to get to TC, and I don't have no money. How am I going to run? She gives me this big roll of bills she says she's been saving for a long time. She says I got to do something. Then she fucks me real good and tells me this is what it could be like every day if she could get away from her old man.'

"Then I ask, Lennie, 'Did she ever say to you directly that she wanted you to kill her husband?'

"He replies, 'Not directly, not like that, but we both knew what she was talking about.'

"I ask, 'Then what happened?' And he replies, 'I took the money and went to that gun shop at Cedar Junction. They had a big display of those AK-47s with a sign that said you should buy one before the law changed. I had enough for one of them and a bunch of ammo.'

"I don't know what you want to do with this," said Ray. "I don't know if this is strong enough to constitute conspiracy."

Tyrrell rocked back and forth slowly in his swivel chair, his elbows resting at the sides of his large, round stomach; he bounced his two hands together, an indication that he was considering the matter. Then he rocked forward and said, "It isn't very strong, Ray. It isn't very strong. Besides, we've clearly got this bastard for murder one, and he's a downstater. Kit's local, and everyone knows she had a tough time. And," he gave Ray a salacious smile, "at least half the men in the area have had a piece of old Kit at some time or another, especially during the time she was a barmaid at the Last Chance. It would not be a popular move on our part, especially right before an election. I'll have to have a word with Jack; we should get her working again, now that she's a widow."

"There's one more thing I want to get your advice on."

"What's that?" asked Tyrrell.

"Grimstock, Roger. That's the man who was killed when his car went off the road."

"What about him?"

"We couldn't find anything at the scene to suggest foul play. I've inspected the car carefully, but it's so banged up I can't prove anything. Still, something doesn't seem right."

"So?" said Tyrrell rocking forward.

"I'd like to go through his cottage and see if there is anything that might tell us something. Do I need a search warrant?"

"Is there anyone there?"

"No. In fact, we haven't found any relatives or friends."

"Well, just go and do it. You're investigating a possible crime. If there's no one around to object, get it done. But Ray, it's summer. Lighten up, you're making work for yourself."

33

"I can't read you the whole autopsy report in a moving car, unless you don't mind my getting car sick." said Sue. "You've read it?" asked Ray

"Yes."

"Just give me a summary, then."

"The two main points are that Grimstock died from a severed spinal cord. The C1 and C2 vertebra were crushed. And his blood alcohol," she continued, "was .21. Given that he was habituated to alcohol, he probably wasn't falling down drunk, but he shouldn't have been driving."

It was beginning to rain and get dark as Ray pulled off the pavement and started down the narrow two-track. The area was low and swampy; tall cattails grew on both sides. The trail rose out of the swamp and ended in a clearing at the edge of a small lake. Ray parked next to the side of the old summerhouse, a square two-story frame building painted dark green with white trim As he and Sue climbed from the car, he had a sense of desolation and decay. Gutters, rotten and collapsing, hung at the sides of the building. The centers of the screens covering the windows and porches had rusted away. The shutters that were still attached tilted at odd angles.

Ray reached back into his car and grabbed a long flashlight. "Let's check the garage first."

Sue followed him to a flat roofed building behind the cottage; its two sets of doors stood open. He found a switch, one of a very old style that turned clockwise and was mounted in a round ceramic fixture. He twisted the switch, nothing happened.

Ray turned on his flashlight. He held the light on the switch. "Look at this," he said to Sue. "This wiring is from the twenties or before. It's called knob and tube. The wires are run separately."

"And it doesn't work," she said in a tone that suggested disinterest.

Ray traced the wires back to a fuse box on the wall at the back of the building. He could see that the main disconnect switch was off. He pushed it into the "on" position. Two bulbs, mounted to the joists above, came on. A late model Audi stood on one side of the garage, the other side was empty. Two bikes, tires flat and covered with rust and cobwebs, leaned against the back wall. Assorted garden tools were piled in a corner near an old, reel-type lawn mower. A golf bag, filled with clubs, slouched against the corner walls.

"This is where he must have parked the Triumph." said Ray looking at the empty stall. "Leaked a lot of oil."

"What exactly are we looking for?" asked Sue.

"I don't know," Ray responded. "I've just got this feeling. Something doesn't seem…"

"What doesn't seem right?"

"He was on the wrong road. Here's a man who gets smashed every night. You'd think that he'd take the shortest way home. He was going way out of his way."

"You're putting yourself in this. If you had too much to drink—if you drove at all, and you probably wouldn't—you would take the most direct route home. What you'd do and what this guy did are two different things…"

Ray protested, "But I've known lots of drunks and they have a homing tendency. It may be at odds with their other self-destructive tendencies, but most of them head for home at the end of the evening. If they don't make it, they're at least going in the right direction. Let's check the house."

Ray turned off the lights. The back door of the cottage was only a few yards from the garage and they ran through the rain, now falling heavily. Ray turned the handle; the door was unlocked. He pushed the door open and felt for the switch. The harsh light from a single bulb illuminated the room. Stacks of empty pizza boxes were spread about the kitchen. Empty beer cans and whiskey bottles were strewn across the counter tops; a large porcelain sink was filled with dirty dishes, glasses, and silverware; the kitchen table was piled with mail.

"Doesn't look like he did trash or dishes," said Sue.

"Or mail," said Ray. "Look at this, none of it has been opened. Like he really didn't care."

"Look at this kitchen," said Sue, "if you need evidence of not caring."

Ray started sorting and stacking the mail.

"Finding anything?" asked Sue.

"Not much, just junk, bills, and this one letter. It's from a bank in Grand Rapids." Ray tore the envelope along the edge and removed the letter. "It's a statement of his trust giving the amount of money currently available from the trust's income." Ray handed her the letter. "Would you call these people, inform them of his death, and see what you can find out about him. Maybe they know if he has an attorney. Let's look through the rest of the place."

They wandered around the old cottage along a narrow trail that ran through the debris. The chaos and decay found in the kitchen continued throughout the house. In the one bedroom that appeared to be in use, the periodic beeping of an answering machine attracted their attention. Ray pushed the "Calls" button; the playback started. It only ran a few seconds. The only sound on the recording was that of a phone being hung up. Ray opened the machine and removed the small tape cassette. He handed it to Sue. "Will you have this tape checked to see if there is anything of interest on it?"

"What do you hope to find?" Sue asked.

"Don't know. But I was able to solve a case because of one of these, years ago when they were a lot less common. It was a murder, much like the Holden murder. Other than the body, we didn't have anything: no motive, no weapon, no physical evidence. On my fifth or sixth trip through the house, I went through the tape and found, buried in a pile of messages, a death threat. The killer was nice enough to give his name."

"You know what Skinner would say?" asked Sue with a smile. "What?"

"Something about how our behavior is shaped by positive reinforcement. And it's true; I proved it to myself running rats in the psych lab."

"Are you comparing me to a rat? I can remember when you used to be nice. Let's get out of here; this place is depressing." Ray turned off lights as they worked their way out of the cottage. He took a key ring off a hook by the door and tried the keys until he found one that opened the back door. He locked the door and handed the key to Sue. "Just in case we need to come back in here."

They dashed through the rain to the car. As Ray dried his glasses he asked, "What did you think?"

"That was awful. I'm not used to looking through other people's things after they are dead. We did this at the Holden's and now here. I almost feel guilty of voyeurism." She paused, "I'm surprised that a building can go for years without maintenance and remain standing. And I guess that I'm equally surprised that Grimstock seemed to get on without taking care of anything."

"It's the Peter Pan approach to life. If you never become an adult, you don't have to take responsibility for anything, The fact that he had a trust fund obviously helped," said Ray. "He didn't have to trouble himself with making a living. He had enough cash for liquor, cigarettes, and whatever."

"But it doesn't look like he lived there. I mean, in spite of the garbage and empty bottles and mail, it doesn't look like he had what you'd call a life."

"That's the tragedy," said Ray, pausing to start the engine. "Most alcoholics will tell you, they just live to drink."

34

Robert Arden was drunk—drunk and angry. He felt the wet grass against his legs as he shuffled toward the beach. The cool wind off the lake stirred the birches overhead; moonlight—variegated, green-gray—came through the clouds and trees to light his way.

The wind surged off Lake Michigan across the few hundred yards of hemlock and pine and onto Loon Lake. The waves on the big lake, widely spaced, tall, and powerful, became short, tight chop on the smaller lake. Whitecaps raced across Loon Lake and broke on its eastern shore.

He dragged the canoe across the grass. A scraping sound resonated along its skin as he pulled it over the sand and gravel beach to the water's edge. When he pushed the canoe into the water, the waves splashed over the bow and forced the craft sideways. With one foot in the canoe and the other on shore, leaning over, each arm holding tight to a side, he shoved off. His weight was off center, the canoe rocked and almost capsized.

He tried paddling from the back, but he couldn't control the canoe in the chop and wind. He carefully crawled forward from the seat, over the cross member, and knelt near the center of the canoe in the cold wash on the bottom. Paddling furiously, he tried to get control of the canoe, turning the bow into the wind, working to hold it there as he made for the small island in the middle of the lake. In spite of his wild stabbing at the water, his progress was slow; strong gusts of wind and the constant surge of the dense chop pushing the canoe off course.

Fifty or sixty yards out, he heard the whine of a starter motor and the snarl of an outboard coming to life on the leeward side of the island. A dark form raced out from the shadows, the wake picking up the moonlight as it approached. The first pass was distant—he could only see the silhouette of the driver; dark, small, leaning close to the wheel. Then the boat came around in a wide circle, slowing, and he could make out the figure. He could see the face clearly in the moonlight; he understood what was happening.

The boat moved away and advanced again at a high speed, veering off at the last second, almost swamping the canoe in its wake. He panicked. For the first time in his life he felt utter and complete terror. He flailed at the water with useless strokes. The canoe was swiped sideways by the wind and a wave rolled over the side, followed by a second, and third. He floated out of the half-submerged canoe. Disoriented, he swam under water, struggling in the dark to find the surface. Once on the surface, he swam for the canoe, but the boat cut him off. Then he could see the canoe being pulled away by the wind and current. Fighting the waves, he started swimming toward the island, only to be cut off by the boat, much larger now that he was in the water. In a panic, he swam furiously, sucking water as he tried to breathe.

He felt the pain first in his left arm. He battled to stay on the surface. Then he felt it in his chest, like a huge fist being driven into him. He stopped struggling and slipped from the moonlight into the dark, cold depths.

35

~~~~~~~~~

Ray found Marc working on his sailboat, shirtless in the late morning sun. He tossed him a small plastic cube. "Here are the Hexagena flies I promised you. The hatch has started, but I don't know when I'm going to get free to go fishing with you and Lisa."

"You don't look like you've seen bed yet."

"At the rate things are going, it doesn't look like I'll get a good night's sleep until the summer is over."

"What kept you up?"

"I spent part of the night helping break up a party. Just when I thought I might be able to go home and get some sleep, I got called to investigate a possible drowning."

"Why didn't you send someone else?"

"I'd left two men out at the scene of the party to make sure it didn't start again, and I'd had just sent home the deputies we got out of bed to help handle the situation. We needed people on the day shift who had had some sleep."

"Big party?"

"Big party, real big party. Hard to tell how many for sure—probably a hundred or more; high school and college kids. Bob was the first on the scene; he came in with siren and lights. He said as soon as the kids saw him, they were running in every direction. The only ones left when I got there were too drunk or stoned to run."

"Where was the party, out at the point?"

"No, but not far from there. It was at one of those expensive new summer homes south of the lighthouse. Some trusting parents left their sweet, little daughter and a friend alone for a few days; two sixteen-year-olds. I got Mom and Dad out of bed —they live in Evanston—told them their daughter had hosted a party, and that we had arrested more than a dozen minors. They were less than thrilled to get the call, especially when I told them a lot of damage had been done to their place."

"What kind of damage?"

"Almost anything that would break—chairs, tables, glasses, even some windows. And barf all over the house. The living room and kitchen are really destroyed. I bet there's ten, fifteen thousand in damage, maybe a lot more. The house is filled with expensive things. This will not be one of the kid's happier memories." Ray paused. "We don't have the manpower to handle this kind of thing: I only have two cars on the road from midnight to seven, and we don't have any place to lock up dozens of drunk, nasty kids."

"So what did you do?"

"The place is on a cul de sac, so after Bob got a sense of what was happening, he blocked off the exit. Most of the cars parked beyond him along the highway quickly disappeared. I was able to get four cars there fairly quickly and we got some help from a state police trooper who was in the area. We ended up sending five kids out by ambulance: three were too intoxicated to talk, and two budding pugilists had nasty facial lacerations and needed stitches. We called in phone numbers to the dispatcher. He got parents out of bed and had them come and pick up their little darlings. We've also got seventeen cars impounded. Before they get their cars back, they'll have to come and talk to us. I imagine some poor bastard tried to go fishing this morning and found that his kid didn't bring the car home last night. There'll be some explaining to do."

"Bet that makes you real popular before an election."

"Doesn't matter, none of them are local."

"So tell me about the other," asked Marc.

"I'm so tired I can't keep on the subject. A call came in about 4:00 a.m. from a woman who thought her husband was out on Loon Lake in a canoe. It was blowing pretty good, and she was worried. I went over and talked with her. Guess they had had an argument and she had gone to bed. Later she woke up and found the house empty. When she went looking for him, she noticed the canoe was gone. I got over there about five. Her story made sense; his car and wallet were there, only the canoe was gone. I called the Coast Guard and they sent a chopper at first light. Found the canoe right away—full of water, caught in some weeds near the dam. The body took a little longer, but they spotted it from the air. It was in about four feet of water near that little island on the south end of the lake. We brought the department's boat over and recovered the body."

"So why was he out in a canoe? It was blowing like hell last night."

"Damned if I know. I'm going to try to get a few hours of sleep, then question her some more and see if we can get a sense of what happened."

"Do you want some coffee?" asked Marc.

"Too tired. I need to get some sleep. Hope we can find a time to go fishing together."

36

When Ray arrived at the Arden cottage, Sue Lawrence was waiting for him. Nancy Arden met them at the door and offered them chairs at the kitchen table.

Arden was holding a drink when they arrived and Ray watched her refresh it; ice cubes and gin in a brandy inhaler. Her speech was slurred and her movements unsteady.

"I'm sorry that I have to ask you more questions, but I want to make sure I have all the information so this matter can be brought to a close as quickly as possible. Would you go back to the beginning and tell me everything that you remember?" asked Ray.

"Well, as I told you this morning, we had a bit of a tiff and I went to bed. Robert was waiting for a call."

"Business?"

"Yes, his assistant was working on some project and was to let him know how things were going. He's been on the phone or hovering over his BlackBerry since we got here. I wonder why he wanted to come. We might as well have stayed in Washington."

"So you went to bed?" continued Ray.

"Yes, I went to bed and woke up about two. The windows were open and the wind had come up. I was cold. I got up to close the windows. Robert hadn't come to bed so I went to look for him. All the lights were on, but he wasn't in the house. The car was here, so I thought he must be walking, but that seemed strange. He doesn't take late night walks. I made some tea and waited for a while. When he didn't show up, I got dressed and went to look for him. That's when I noticed the canoe was gone. It was really blowing. I got scared and called…"

"You said you had a "tiff," you were arguing?"

"Yes."

"And were you both drinking?"

"Yes."

"About how many drinks did your husband have?"

"He was drinking Scotch. I wasn't counting. I don't know; six or seven, perhaps more."

"Over what period of time?"

Arden didn't answer immediately. "Can't say for sure—two, three hours."

Ray asked, "Was your husband intoxicated?"

"I think we were both pretty far gone."

"Why did you think to check on the canoe?"

"He just bought it, hand built, spent a fortune on it. It was one of the things that we were arguing about. I thought if he really wanted to make me angry, he might go canoeing with a storm blowing.

"And you're sure no one was with him?"

"Yes. We're here alone. People don't just drop in after midnight."

"How long have you been here?"

"We flew in on Saturday; we haven't been here for several years. He was always too busy to take a week or two off. Suddenly, late last week, he had this urgent need to come up here. I called and had the place opened. We have a local handy man that looks after the place. Robert had to pull some strings to get us seats to T.C. on a summer weekend."

"Do you know why he had such a need to come?" Ray asked.

"I thought he was tired and tense and just wanted to get away. But he never settled down when he got here," she replied. "He seemed even more tense."

"Tense about what?"

"He was always tense. He was tense about everything—tense about the Democrats, tense about the press, tense the V.P. would make another major..."

"Could you tell me about your husband's job?"

"Not much to tell, and kind of hard to explain. He works for the White House as a special assistant for media relations. His job was feeding the media the administration's view of the world." She paused. "That isn't quite correct. His job was to create or interpret events in a way that made the administration look good. He also did damage control when something happened that was perceived to put the administration in a bad light."

There was a long pause. She opened a new pack of cigarettes, slowly, trying to steady her hands. She removed one, lit it, and inhaled deeply. She lifted her head, blew a stream of smoke toward the ceiling, and raised the cigarette to her lips again.

Ray, feeling embarrassed by the long silence, asked, "Were you married long?"

"Twenty-five years. We met at Albion. Robert was this handsome fellow from a wealthy, politically connected family. As I look back, I was an incredibly naive, provincial kid—my father was a Methodist minister in Saginaw. I remember the first time he took me home; his family lived in Virginia, just outside Washington. They had two Monets in the dining room, a Picasso in the living room, maids in uniforms—I didn't know people really lived like that. I was impressed by it all and too dumb to see anything but the glitter. We got married after graduation, and he went on to GW law school. His family bought us this lovely row house in Georgetown, and he had a large trust fund. It was a real Cinderella story. I was going to teach school. But soon after we married I got pregnant. I had our second child before he finished law school.

"After he got his law degree, he got a job in the administration. At first I thought he was wonderfully idealistic, but he changed over the years. He had a kind of political paranoia. He would tell me about things he was involved with that were clearly unethical, and perhaps illegal.

"When I confronted him, he would justify his actions by saying that they had to be done to prevent the liberals from getting control of the White House and that the Democrats did the same thing.

"About that time I also became aware of his first affair, or I think it was his first affair. I was so stupid; I blamed myself." She took a long sip of her drink and finished it. She continued telling her story as she made herself another drink.

"The fairy tale ended. That was the end of my innocence and the beginning of my education. I should have divorced him then, but I wasn't strong enough; I had two babies. And finally after all of these years, now that the kids are out, I was strong enough. I was going to tell him this week I was leaving. Even in the end he cheated me." She paused, her tone changed. "The kids are flying in this evening. I don't know how to act. I'm sorry you had to listen to all of this; I just had to talk."

"I understand." Ray waited to see if she was finished. When it was clear she was, he began. "There are a few more questions I would like to ask if you feel you're up to it."

"Go ahead," she said. "I'm sorry I rambled so."

"This is a hard question to ask, but I must," said Ray. "Do you have any reason to suspect that your husband might have been depressed or suicidal?"

"Not at all. He was a workaholic. He felt needed. Suicide doesn't fit. He was often upset, but I don't think depressed. He seemed to thrive on tension and chaos. I don't think he was introspective enough to ever consider suicide."

"What I'm struggling with, Mrs. Arden, is why your husband was in the canoe last night, especially considering the weather."

"I can't explain it, Sheriff. It doesn't make sense to me. As I said, maybe he was doing it for spite. During our argument I teased him about spending so much on a canoe when he hadn't even used one since he was a kid. Maybe he was trying to show me something, or just worry me."

Ray nodded, not satisfied with her answer. Then he offered, "If you're going to be alone until your children get here, I could have Deputy Lawrence stay with you if that would help."

"No, I've got a rental car. I'm going to town to pick them up. In fact, I need to leave for the airport fairly soon."

"Why don't I have Deputy Lawrence drive you to the airport to pick them up? Would that help?"

"Yes, I guess I really shouldn't be driving."

"The medical examiner should be done sometime today. Do you want to know the results of the autopsy?" Ray asked.

"Yes, please. When can we…?" she started to cry.

"The body?"

She nodded to Ray's question.

"It should be released after the autopsy, late this afternoon. If you need anything, please call, and we'll try to help."

37

It was early evening by the time Ray reached the Bussey House. He had called earlier and arranged the meeting.

He drove up the long, paved drive to the house. The garage door was open; a Jaguar XJS and a Range Rover sat side by side, both with Illinois plates.

He was greeted at the front door by the same young woman who had met him on his first visit. She escorted him into the living room and offered him a seat. After she left, he got up and walked to the windows facing the lake. The doorwalls were open and a warm breeze came off the lake. Ray noted the second movement of Mozart's *Clarinet Concerto* was playing softly in the background. The sun had already dropped into the water; only the top quarter remained above the surface. And, as he watched, that quarter disappeared. The area continued to glow, brightly at first and then gradually diminishing; the margins of the horizon had already turned to gray.

Ray felt her presence and turned. Mrs. Bussey was standing behind him.

"You seemed so lost in thought I didn't want to disturb you," she offered quietly. She seemed softer and less brittle then on their first encounter. With a gesture toward the center of the room, she directed Ray to a sofa. He settled at one end. She sat on its twin, a glass-topped coffee table separated them.

"I was enjoying watching the sun disappear. I don't take time often enough to do things like that. You have a wonderful view."

"It is grand, isn't it," she responded in a relaxed tone. Ray noted a tranquility about her.

"I doubt, however, that you are here to talk about sunsets and the view," her voice took on a business-like tone. "How can I be of assistance?"

"Well, as you no doubt suspected, it's about your former husband. When the investigators from the Michigan Fire Marshall's office went through the remains of the boat, they found several sticks of dynamite. The dynamite appeared to have been hidden in the engine compartment. As the boat sank, that area filled first with water, protecting the dynamite from the heat and fire. If it had exploded, other people would probably have died. I realize that you and Mr. Bussey have been divorced for several years, but do you know of anyone who might have wanted to kill him?"

"I am sure there were many people who wouldn't have minded seeing him dead. Arthur was devious and unencumbered by ethics, business or otherwise. He used to say that business was war, and if you wanted to succeed you had to be willing to do anything to gain your end. He never allowed friendship or sentimentality to get in his way. Not only did he do in many of his friends, but he liked to brag about it." She paused. "However, to answer your question, I don't know if anyone was angry enough to actually kill him. But I can tell you about the dynamite."

"Go on," Ray responded.

"Well, I am a little surprised he was still doing that. He used to do that when we had the other boat, the smaller one. He would get dynamite from one of his construction sites. When we were out cruising—and I think only when we had some of his guests on board whom he wanted to impress—he would go out in the inflatable and throw weighted sticks in the water and collect any fish that floated up." She raised her eyebrows, and with a voice tinged with sarcasm she continued, "He was a real sportsman, that one." She paused again and her tone changed. "Were you surprised to find me here?"

"I'm not following," responded Ray.

"Today was Arthur's funeral. I guess it was bad form not to go back for it. I should have appeared in ex-wife weeds. But, then, his people aren't my people. For me, it's finally over."

"What's that?"

"All the turmoil caused by the divorce; the marriage was over, but he was still around. It was like an open wound that continued to ooze. Now it is over; that part of my life is closed. I can get on with things." She gave Ray a rather tenuous smile and continued, "I saw on the news tonight we had a drowning."

"Yes. We seem to have two or three each summer. This was the first."

"I was only half listening, but I heard the name Robert Arden... Is that right?"

"Yes. We recovered his body this morning. Apparently he was canoeing during the night and capsized. Did you know him?"

"I met him, years ago. He was a high school friend of Arthur's and a summer friend up here. He got married about the same time we did. We used to do things together years ago. I bet we haven't seen them in twenty years. Was he up here with a wife?"

"Yes."

"I wonder if it was the same wife?" The tone of her voice suggested an internal speculation that she verbalized without thinking.

"I have talked with the victim's wife. I believe she is the first wife."

"I liked her a lot, but I could never see them as a couple. She was very sweet—dreadfully naive, but very sweet. I enjoyed her. But I hated the way the two men acted when we got together. They seemed to bring out the worst in each other, they acted like adolescents." She paused. "You know, I could never see them as a couple."

"Why not?" asked Ray. He didn't really want to get involved in gossip, but her comment begged a response.

"She was so dear, so innocent. And Robert was so sleazy. It was hard to understand. He was from a solid family, old money, good people. I just didn't think she quite knew what was going on. They had babies right away and we lost track of them. I'm surprised they were still together." She paused. "There is a bit of a coincidence here, isn't there?"

"I guess there is." Ray thought about it for a moment and then getting up said, "Thank you for your time, Mrs. Bussey. And thank you for helping to clear my question about the explosives."

"I am glad to help, Sheriff. If there is anything else, please call." She escorted him to the door. He noticed that she was still standing there looking after him as he turned to get into his car.

38

Marc sat on the deck drinking coffee, his dog sleeping at his side. There had been no sunrise, just heavy gray clouds that took on a yellowish-purple tint at the appropriate time. The air was still and close. The lake, mirror-like, reflected the color of the sky. The leaves on the poplars, oaks, and maples that lined the lake, even at their tops, were motionless. It was the stillness that often precedes a summer storm. Only the birds disturbed the quiet with their usual morning cacophony of calls and whistles.

Marc heard the car approach through the woods. He poured some coffee into an extra cup and waited for Ray to come around the side of the cottage. "You look almost awake this morning," he greeted.

"Well, I finally got some sleep. I've never had a week like this—never. Did you go fishing last night?"

"No, we went to a concert and came home and read. We saw you on the 11:00 news."

"What did you think, or more importantly, what did Lisa think?"

"I thought you did fine. You'll have to ask Lisa what she thought. You didn't give any extra information, that's for sure," offered Marc.

"Just the facts. You have to be so damn careful you don't say anything that will come back to haunt you later."

"You were clear; you were articulate, and you looked good on camera. What more could you ask for?"

The screen door slammed and Lisa joined them.

"We were just talking about Ray's appearance on the news. He's interested in your impression; I have already given him my unschooled opinion of how well he McLuhanized us viewers."

Lisa pulled a chair up to the table as Marc filled a cup for her. Ray was struck by the fact that she was wearing glasses.

"Are we discussing media manipulation again?" she asked with a half smile and then stretched languorously.

"Serious question," said Ray.

"You did fine. You seemed competent and in control of the situation. I think that is exactly the image you want to project. And now that you're dressing for success…"

"You ask a serious question," said Ray, "and what do you get? Sarcasm."

"Relax," said Lisa with a smile, "you done good. And compared with the reporter and the local anchorman, you looked like the only real professional—they don't seem to get major-market talent up here."

"It's much better than it used to be," said Marc. He continued, "You're getting more TV time than you expected."

"Too damn much," said Ray. "It always gets busy in the summer, but never like this. We got a whole summer's worth of death and destruction in a week. I hope this is the end of it, but you summer people just keep things hopping."

"Something new?" asked Marc.

"No, just a complication of an old case. Remember that party we had to break up the other night? Did Marc tell you about it?" He looked at Lisa and she nodded affirmatively. "One of the boys, who apparently caused most of the destruction, told the girl whose house he tore up that if she identified him, he and his friends would gang rape her. Her parents want her to name names, but she refuses to cooperate. She's convinced that the guys are going to get her if she talks. Right now the parents are mad at me because we don't know who the boys are…"

Marc interrupted, "I thought you caught a lot of the kids at the scene."

"We did, those who were too drunk to run. The boys who did the real damage had cleared out before we got there. If Mandy, that's her name, would help, it would sure speed things up. But she is absolutely hysterical."

Lisa began, her voice forceful: "You guys don't understand how vulnerable women feel. And the fact that these boys would threaten her makes me furious."

"You don't take a threat like that seriously. They were trying to scare her," said Ray.

"No, you don't; men don't take something like that seriously," said Lisa with anger in her voice. "But women always have to take it seriously. Women are always vulnerable to attack—and their attackers are not other women. From the time I was a little girl I knew that I had to be careful in ways the boys didn't. When I was in college I had two friends who were raped. One by a hockey player who thought anyone accepting a date with him was giving consent. The other girl was grabbed walking back to the house from the library—they never caught the guy. If you could see what those girls went through, you would understand my anger."

"Lisa, I didn't mean to suggest that rape isn't serious. And if it sounded like that, I'm sorry. What I meant was that these threats are just a ruse to keep her quiet. Teenage boys often get swept away with their own bravado and say things they don't mean. On the other hand, I would like to get the boys and nail them to the wall for these threats and the damage they did to that house."

Lisa softened, "You didn't deserve that much anger from me—I've just seen too many women damaged. I understand why that girl is scared. I really hope you get those bastards."

"We'll get them," said Ray, "it's just gonna take more time than I hoped. We are questioning some of the other kids who were at the party. But, if we can leave this discussion of youthful violence, I want to pick your brains."

"More cunning campaign tactics?" asked Lisa, attempting to lighten the conversation."

"No, this has to do with coincidences, too many coincidences," said Ray.

"Go ahead, give us your coincidences. We need something in addition to the coffee to get our brains going this morning," offered Marc.

"Well, last night I stopped to see the ex-wife of Arthur Bussey. Several sticks of dynamite were found hidden in the engine compartment of what was left of his sailboat. I stopped to ask if she knew of anyone who might want to off her ex. It seems that he used the stuff for fishing."

"I don't understand," said Lisa.

Ray looked over at Marc with a knowing smile. "Marc does, ask him to explain it."

"This one I want to hear about," said Lisa.

"It's not much of a story. It happened when we were about sixteen or seventeen. Ray borrowed—he used to say liberated—some dynamite from his uncle's farm. His uncle used dynamite to remove tree stumps."

"I like the way you tell the story as if I did all the doing," said Ray. "You were with me every step of the way."

"Let me correct the story. We borrowed some dynamite—two sticks—because we had heard that it was a good way to see how many trout were in a hole."

Lisa looked perplexed, "I'm not following."

"Well, the idea is that you throw some weighted sticks of dynamite into a deep hole, and the trout are stunned by the concussion and float to the surface."

"Did it work?"

"We didn't have the facts straight," continued Marc. "The explosion turned out to be a hell of a lot bigger than we had planned. Water, weeds, logs, and sand went flying every which way. It scared the hell out of us. If there had been any trout in that hole, well, they were paté after the blast. And the blast cured us of any further experimentation."

"That's a great story. You're lucky you didn't get hurt or killed."

Ray nodded in affirmation. "I think that we both recognized that, although I doubt if either of us mentioned it. But let me get back to the widow, I mean, the ex-wife of Arthur Bussey. She said something that was very interesting. I guess that I had been thinking about it, but her talking about it really made me consider it seriously."

"What's that?" asked Lisa.

"Well, she mentioned that she saw the drowning story—Robert Arden who drowned over on Loon Lake. She mentioned that her ex and Arden had been friends up here when they were in their teens. She also said that when they and the Ardens were young marrieds, they had spent time together."

"So what's so remarkable about that?" Lisa queried.

"Nothing, absolutely nothing. But it got me to thinking. We have our share of people getting hurt and killed here. And in the summer it's much worse because the population more than doubles. Every summer we have two or three drownings, a number of deaths with cars and motorcycles, and an occasional murder—usually the murders involve locals. But this year the summer barely has started and we've already had two murders—Hammer and Holden—a drowning, a traffic death, and someone killed by lightning."

"Unusual," said Marc, "but not statistically improbable."

"Yes, but there is something unusual. The last four were all in their forties. They were all summer people, and they all spent time up here when they were kids."

"It's an interesting coincidence," said Marc. "And given our age, gender, and so forth," he flicked his finger back and forth pointing at Ray and then himself, "a rather frightening coincidence. But it's not like you have four murders. It is not like someone was out there knocking off forty-something fudgies."

"That's true," Ray responded. "Only one of the four was murder. But..."

"What are you implying?" probed Lisa.

"I'm not sure I'm implying anything yet. But I was struck by the coincidences. We had one murder, right? Then we had someone die as the result of lightning hitting his boat—pretty hard to arrange. But look at the last two. A guy drives off the road in the rain, and another fellow falls out of his canoe and drowns."

"What about the last two?" asked Marc. "I don't see what you are getting at."

"Let me give you this scenario. Let's say someone wanted to kill a number of people. Using a gun, like in the first murder, is highly effective but not particularly imaginative. Now take Roger Grimstock, the fellow who drove off the road. Let's say someone wanted him dead. They could have run him off the road knowing that the chances of him getting killed were pretty good. There's no other place in the county where the sides of the road are steeper, and it's about the only place where there aren't adequate barriers."

"I haven't heard you say you have evidence to support this kind of speculation," said Marc.

"Wait, there's more. Grimstock was drinking at the Last Chance the night he died, he drank there every night during the summer. Jack Grochoski—he's the bartender, owns the place—told me that the night of the accident Grimstock got a phone call. Jack says that's the first phone call Grimstock's gotten since his wife left him years ago."

"Interesting," opined Marc, "but it hardly proves anything."

"There's one more interesting fact. The accident took place way over on Ely Road—that's not on the way to the Grimstock cottage.

"But Ray, you have to admit that none of this is particularly unusual. There are, no doubt, perfectly logical explanations for these events," said Marc, "and if you could only question the late Mr. Grimstock, I'm sure your suspicions…"

"Perhaps, but there is also the Arden drowning that has some strange circumstances. A guy buys an expensive canoe. His wife says she doesn't think he's been canoeing since he was a kid. And when he does decide to go for a paddle, it's in the middle of the night when the wind is up and the lake is rougher than hell. It seems damn strange, that's all."

"I think I've got it." said Lisa. "A humanist interested in helping to control the over-supply of middle-aged, white males is doing some selective harvesting? Perhaps we just have a Darwinist trying to improve the quality of the breeding stock by eliminating some of the old bucks."

"Careful, love," said Marc, "you are getting too close to home. If your theory is correct, Ray and I could be next."

"I am sure no one could feel that way about you or Ray. There's always a need to protect rare vintages."

"Here's another possibility. Someone is trying to do something about the glass ceiling."

"You're a real wit, aren't you?" said Ray. "I bring a complicated problem to a couple of old friends with the expectation that they will help me think it through, and what do I get—some smart-assed…"

"Hold on Ray," said Lisa. "I'll be serious and talk this through with you. You've got four dead guys, all white, middle-aged, middle class, and college educated. What else would you want to know about them?"

"I would want to know if they had criminal records, their sources of income, net worth, whether they were involved in any civil actions, who they owed money to…"

"Mutual acquaintances, if any," interjected Lisa.

"That's a good one," said Marc. "Did they know one another?"

"Based on what Mrs. Bussey told me," said Ray, "Arthur Bussey knew Robert Arden when they were in their teens and early twenties. And they came from families who had cottages in the area. Given that they are about the same age, it's quite possible that they were all acquainted."

"Did they go to the same colleges?" asked Lisa.

Marc offered, "Randy Holden went to Michigan; he was there at the same time I was."

"Well," said Ray, "Jenson's ex said they went to Northwestern, and Arden's widow said they met at Albion. Grimstock, I don't know. I'll have to check."

"Have we helped?" Lisa asked.

"Yeah, I just have to do the leg work to see if any of the pieces fit."

39

Nancy Arden met Ray at the back door and ushered him in. As they walked through the kitchen, she introduced him to her son, Robert Jr., and daughter, Amy, who were busy cooking hamburgers. Ray noted that the son was tall, thin and appeared to be in his early twenties. The daughter was the younger, but there was a striking resemblance between the two: their hair color, their eyes, their facial features. Ray assumed they looked more like their father, although he didn't have a clear idea what the father looked like when he was alive, only the image of the body pulled from the lake.

Nancy led him through the cottage to the front porch that faced the lake. They made small talk for a few minutes as people invariably do when there are serious matters to discuss, but a reluctance to approach them.

Finally, Ray broached the subject for his visit. "I wanted to see you before you left. I think I told you I would call with the autopsy results, but I thought it better if I delivered them in person. You're still interested in knowing?"

"Yes, please, go ahead."

"Well, as expected, he had a lot of water in his lungs, but it doesn't appear that was the cause of death. The pathologist said the immediate cause of death was a massive heart attack. Did your husband have a history of heart trouble?"

"No, not that I know of. There were a lot of things he kept from me, but I think he would have told me about any major health problems. I know he was concerned about his cholesterol, and he kept trying to give up smoking. But I don't think he had ever had any symptoms. He just had the same health concerns other men his age have."

"Well," said Ray "this makes me wonder whether he had the heart attack and the canoe capsized, or if the canoe capsized and he had the heart attack trying to swim to shore. There was another interesting finding."

"What was that, Sheriff?"

"Well, he had a high level of blood alcohol, point one eight. In fact, in Michigan that's almost twice the legal limit."

"As I told you before, Sheriff, we had both had a lot to drink."

"I guess I was wondering whether that might have contributed to the accident. Would Robert have gone canoeing in those conditions if he had been sober?"

"I don't know how to answer you. Robert liked to drink. I wouldn't say he was an alcoholic, but he did drink. Most of those in his circle of friends drank a lot. Even when he was drinking quite heavily, he was always articulate and seemed to be in control. I guess you would say that he could hold his liquor. That doesn't mean he wasn't cautious, sometimes too cautious I thought."

"How's that?" asked Ray.

"When he was drinking he made a point of not driving. There were lots of times when we left cars at restaurants and parties and took a cab home. It was inconvenient. The next day he would take my car to the office and I was expected to retrieve his."

Ray paused a moment and looked thoughtful. "Given what you have just told me about his not wanting to drive when he had been drinking, I don't understand why he would be out in a canoe at night in heavy winds."

"He wouldn't have thought about the two things in the same way. Getting charged with driving drunk would have a damaging effect on his career and be an embarrassment to the administration. Not the same thing."

Ray couldn't quite follow her logic, but he didn't pursue the point. "How are your children dealing with their father's death?"

"They are finding it confusing."

"Confusing?" asked Ray.

"Yes, confusing. They haven't ever been really close to their father—he was never around. Recently, their relationship with him became extremely tenuous. One evening last year my daughter was in Georgetown with some friends and spotted her father's car in a parking lot; it was hard to miss, he had vanity plates with his initials. It was a new BMW and she took her friends over to look at it. Robert was in the car with a woman. She would never tell me exactly what they were doing, but it doesn't take much imagination. It was just awful for Amy. I guess she caused a big scene in the parking lot and her friends had to drag her away. You can't imagine how destructive that was. She's been in counseling ever since, I think only recently has finally started to get through it. Robert Jr. has hardly said a word to his father since he heard about it. That is why we came up here alone. The kids didn't want to be any place where they have to be close to him. And now they're confused because he's dead, and they don't feel sorry. I guess Robert's last act as a father was to make them feel guilty."

Ray sat quietly. He wanted to respond but didn't know quite what to say.

"Sheriff, there was something else I wanted to tell you. I think you asked if anything was bothering Robert. It didn't strike me as important at the time, but perhaps it was. The second or third day we were here there was a report in the paper about the man who was killed when his car left the road."

"Yes, his name was Roger Grimstock," Ray offered.

"Robert read the story and seemed bothered by it. I asked him if he knew the man, and he said he had years ago when they were teenagers. I asked if they had been friends. He said no, he didn't really like him, he just knew him. But I do remember that the story seemed to upset him. He mentioned later that he hoped the fellow had been killed instantly because it would be awful to die alone. I guess it doesn't mean anything. I just thought it was interesting."

"It is, thank you for telling me," said Ray.

"Sheriff, there's one more thing."

"Yes."

"I wanted to thank you for having the deputy take me to the airport. I guessed you recognized I shouldn't have been driving. I'm glad you did." She looked out at the lake. "This all must be very hard for the kids; it's confusing for me, too. I don't know how to act at the funeral. I don't want to be false." She paused and looked at Ray. "You have helped a lot Sheriff. You've listened when I needed someone to listen. Thank you for that."

"I'm glad we could help. If there's anything else we can do for you, and your children, please call."

She walked him back through the cottage to the door. Robert and Amy were sitting at the kitchen table eating quietly as they passed.

40

The sign had three neon waves, royal blue with crests of white that blazed in slow succession to suggest the dance of whitecaps rolling to shore. Over the waves, hot pink neon letters in a stylized script proclaimed The Third Wave, each word flashing on as the wave below it illuminated until all three words were lit. The name would glow for several seconds after the last wave faded, then dim until the whole process began again moments later.

André and Mr. Charles, the proprietors of The Third Wave, were new to the area. They had purchased the only beauty shop in the village in late fall, and had spent most of the winter renovating both the interior and exterior. The building housing the business, dating back to the twenties, had originally been a filling station and was converted it to a beauty shop in the late fifties. After Betty—of Betty's Beauty Nook—passed away, the building stood empty.

When The Third Wave first opened in early April, the local women were pleased to have a beauty shop in the village again, but didn't know quite what to make of André and Mr. Charles. They dressed identically in skin-tight black pants and loose white canvas pullovers that opened in a "V" to mid-chest. They wore matching hair styles, carefully shaped and tinted. And their sandal-covered feet showed the extensive nature of their rich tans.

The new interior of The Third Wave left no traces of Betty's Beauty Nook. The reception area had been expanded, and André and Mr. Charles now worked their miracles in the area that had once held a grease pit and service bay. The large aluminum coffee urn had been replaced by a silver tea service, and the coffee now had a hint of cinnamon, chocolate, or almonds. Foam cups had been supplanted by Belleek cups and saucers. A neat pile of delicate linen napkins was renewed throughout the day. The floor, once covered in maroon vinyl, was now a lustrous pink marble. The walls were papered in subtle pastels, and the windows cloaked in elegant lace.

While the women of the village found the "boys"—that's the way they were referred to locally—"a bit much," the women from Birmingham, Grosse Pointe, West Bloomfield, and Winnetka were comforted to find a bit of home when they came north for the summer.

As Lisa sat waiting to get her hair cut she tried to interest herself in the current issues of *House Beautiful, House and Garden, People, Town and Country,* and *Redbook.* She finally settled on looking at the pictures in *Architectural Digest.* She glanced up briefly as another woman came in and settled into a chair across from her in the waiting area. She glanced up a second time as the woman sorted through the pile of magazines. Lisa thought the woman looked vaguely familiar. She couldn't immediately place her. The woman looked back, and Lisa could tell she was also struggling.

"Hello, you look quite familiar, I'm Lisa Alworth."

"I was thinking, too, that you looked familiar. Is that a married name?"

"Yes, Weston was my maiden name."

The woman looked thoughtful. "Lisa Weston, that sounds more familiar. Now I know who you are. You were a pledge my senior year. I'm Marilyn Case; I was Marilyn Holden then."

"I remember you… You were Missy Morrison's big sister, weren't you?" asked Lisa.

"Yes, I haven't thought of her in years. Ann Arbor seems like another life now, doesn't it? We grow up."

"Or at least we get older," said Lisa with a wry smile.

"I remember about you too; you were a bit of a wit. You never seemed to take any of the hocus-pocus of the sorority seriously. You were one of the more interesting pledges. I take it you're married and have a summer place in the area."

"The name is left over from a starter marriage. I should have changed it back. But you're right on the second count. My family has a place here. And you?"

"My husband and I just bought a condo on the peninsula. I've loved it here, been coming up here since I was a child. My parents had a place on the big lake."

"Are you up for the whole summer?" asked Lisa.

"Yes, I came up as soon as the kids were out of school. Had to go back for a few days for a funeral; came back up last night."

"No one close, I hope."

"Yes and no. It was my older brother, but we were hardly close."

Lisa made the connection between Marilyn's maiden name and Randy Holden. She was chagrined and didn't know what to say next.

Marilyn continued, "I'm sure you heard about it. It was big news up here. He was shot."

"Yes, just as you said that it occurred to me that your brother might have been the victim. It must have been a horrible thing for…"

"It was unpleasant, but not surprising. My one reservation about buying the condo in this area was that I might have to run into him. I don't think we had talked in five or six years, not since my father died."

"Why weren't you surprised?"

"Randy was a low life, a cheat, a scoundrel, a rake." She enunciated each derisive term with great care and vehemence. She continued, her tone lightening. "And he was handsome, polished, and extremely charming. He used everyone, always had. I imagine this time he conned the wrong person and got himself killed. From the time we were kids he was always in some kind of trouble. My parents were two of the most ethical and proper people you could find. Randy caused them endless grief. And they did everything they could: made sure he got a good education, helped get him jobs, covered bad checks, and helped him get out of trouble numerous times. I think they finally gave up on him. Thank God they didn't live long enough to see this."

"What kind of trouble?"

"It wasn't like he stole hubcaps. He was always a confidence man, always taking people in and then using them. By the time he was in high school there were already major problems. I was much younger, and my parents tried to keep me in the dark about what was going on. I just knew that every time there was a major crisis at home, Randy was in some new difficulty."

"But you don't know exactly…"

"Not the early problems, I was kept ignorant of those. Later, when he was working as a lawyer, well—that was in all the papers. My mother once told me that a psychiatrist friend said that Randy had a sociopathic personality—she didn't really understood what the psychiatrist was telling her. From that point on she felt better about Randy because she didn't think he was responsible for his misdeeds; his problems were caused by some illness. That's when I was a junior or senior in college, a psych major. I didn't have the heart to tell her those big words just meant Randy was a sleaze-bag with a criminal mind."

"And the funeral?"

"I didn't want to go. But one of my father's oldest friends, a man who was his law partner for over forty years, called and reminded me that my parents would want me to do the proper thing, regardless of what my brother did to me. This man handled my parents' estate, knew my brother screwed me out of the family cottage, among other things. But he wanted to make sure I did the 'proper' thing. I met the new wife—a very young woman—and worked with her to plan the funeral. She was really nice; I liked her a lot. That was one of the amazing things about Randy. He was always able to attract interesting women. Once they figured him out, they got out, but it didn't take him long to come up with another one."

"Sounds like a real charmer," said Lisa sarcastically.

"That's a good name for him, a charmer. Anyway, that's finished, and I can get on with the summer. It's good we've finally got a decent beauty shop, isn't it? Betty didn't understand hair."

Mr. Charles came out with a client and entered her bill on the cash register. After he was paid and tipped, he walked her to her car.

Before Lisa could be ushered in, Marilyn offered, "It's good to see you. I think I would like to know you as an adult. If you can stand two middle-school boys, I'd love to have you over for lunch. I'll write our number on the back of a card." She took one of the salon's business cards—neon blue letters on a hot pink background—from the counter, and wrote down her number.

"I would like that," Lisa said, taking the card. "I'll call you early next week."

"Good," said Marilyn, "I'm looking forward to seeing you again."

41

The sound of the car door brought Claire Lapointe out onto the back porch: a slender, sinewy woman in her late seventies, with gray-black hair pulled back into a bun, and thin, wire-rimmed glasses perched below the bridge of a delicate nose. Ray remembered how his mother used to bring him along as a boy when she would visit Claire. He remembered how strikingly beautiful she used to be. She was still a beautiful woman.

"Thanks for coming, Ray," she said as she came down the porch steps. "Dad's in the barn working on something. He just won't let go of this. He's convinced that someone moved that old truck, and he keeps going on and on about it."

"You don't think it was moved?" asked Ray.

"Look, Ray, he doesn't seem to remember hardly anything from one day to the next. The boys just don't appreciate what I have to put up with. They just think I'm going on about how forgetful Dad is. He hasn't used the truck since last fall. I'm surprised it even starts. How would he remember where he left it? Half the time he can't remember where to get a clean pair of shorts. I've been putting them in the same drawer for over fifty years. But humor him, Ray. Humor him."

Ray walked to the barn. It was empty. He followed the sound of a motor to the next building, a small garage. John stood in front of an electric grinder. A shower of sparks came from the piece of steel he was holding against the grinding wheel. Ray walked to one side and grabbed his elbow. John jumped. He switched off the grinder. "You scared the hell out of me, Ray."

"Sorry, I didn't mean to surprise you."

"Thanks for coming. Someone's been messing with my truck, and that old woman," John said, irritation in his voice and pointing toward the house, "just don't believe me."

"Show me the truck," said Ray.

John led him behind the garage. "Last fall I mounted the snowplow and left it sit right here. Look where the grass grew long. That's where it sat. I come back here yesterday and the truck is over here. Just ten feet over, but over here. And there is one more thing, Ray, I topped off the tank last fall so it would be ready to go. Now more than a quarter of a tank is gone. Tell me that someone didn't take the truck."

"And you never used the truck to plow snow?"

"No, I wanted to, but the old woman," he motioned toward the house again, "she won't let me. She hired young Bob Johnson down the road. She said she didn't want me dying of a heart attack just to save a few dollars on snowplowing. She don't let me do anything anymore."

"Could one of the boys have borrowed the truck?"

"No, I checked. I called Junior just to see if he took it. I sometimes forget things, you know what I mean? He said he hadn't used it for several years. And Bobby is working downstate. He hasn't been up here for several months."

"I didn't know Bobby had moved," said Ray.

"He got transferred downstate sometime in early spring. He didn't want to move, but the manager of the Detroit branch had a heart attack and they needed him. He's hoping the guy will get better so he can move back."

"When did you notice the truck had been moved?" Ray asked.

"Yesterday morning. I came back here looking for something, and I knew something was wrong. You know how that is. At first I thought I must be confused, but as soon as I walked over here and saw this pattern in the grass, I knew that it had been moved."

"Other than the missing gas, the truck hasn't been damaged or vandalized in any way."

"Not that I can tell. I took it for a little drive and everything seems to work all right."

Ray walked around the truck looking for new damage. The sheet metal on the old truck was covered with dings and rust holes. Ray inspected the snow blade, held by a hydraulic piston about a foot off the ground. He noted that in two places the coating of rust that uniformly covered the surface of the blade had been scratched away, exposing bare metal.

"John, when you took your test drive, you didn't push anything with the blade, did you?"

John came to his side; Ray pointed to the gashes on the blade.

"To be truthful, Ray, I didn't notice those. See what I tell you, someone did use this truck. When you go back, stop at the house and tell the old lady about this. Every time I tell her something, she says I'm just getting old and funny. Tell her, will you?"

"I'll stop and have a word. And I'm going to send my evidence technician to check the truck for prints. She's a young, pretty woman, John. You'll like talking to her. She'll have to take your prints, too."

"Mine?"

"She has to be able to tell the difference between your prints and any others that might be in your truck. Don't touch the truck again until she is finished, understand?"

"I hear you. I won't go near the damn thing till you're done with it."

"When I get back in the car, I'll call in. She'll probably be here tomorrow morning. I've got to run."

"You will stop at the house and tell her, Ray?"

"Yes, I'll stop and have a word with your wife. I promise," said Ray.

42

Dell was standing outside the garage having a cigarette as Ray approached.

"Cigarette, Sheriff?"

"I quit."

"Another one, hardly any of us left anymore."

"Time to give it up, Dell. Those things can kill you."

"Look Sheriff, a whole lot of things have been trying to kill me. Nothing's done it yet. At this point I've outlived most of my friends. A few cigarettes won't make a hell of a lot of difference."

"I want to look at that Triumph again."

Dell walked with him to the fenced storage area.

"What are you looking for?"

"I want to see if there is any sign that the car was hit by something, something like the blade of a snowplow."

Dell walked around the car with Ray.

"I can tell you one thing, Sheriff. It wasn't a head-on. The front bumper and grill are the only things that aren't busted up."

Ray walked around to the rear of the car. "What happened to the back bumper?"

"It wasn't there when the car was brought in. When the rear slammed into that tree, it probably got torn off." Dell looked from one side to the other. "You can see how the damn thing was attached. Fucking limey engineering. Bumpers on their cars were too damn flimsy to do any good. This one probably caught on the tree. You can see where the bolt pulled through the sheet metal. You got two broken studs back here, and the sheet metal is torn on the other side. Those bumpers were never anything more than trim, anyway. They didn't have any strength. I'm glad these damn cars aren't around anymore; they were a royal pain in the ass to work on. Five pounds of shit in a three-pound bag, you know what I mean? Five pounds of shit in a three- pound bag. You could never get the damn things to run right."

"Dell, where is the rear bumper?"

"It still may be in the woods somewhere. If Jeff threw it on the truck, it would've been stacked with the scrap over there." He motioned with his hand. "Company from Grand Rapids has a truck come through once a month and pick it up. He was here yesterday. If your bumper was in that pile, it's gone now."

"Dell, I told you to hold onto the car until we were through with the investigation."

"Car's there, Sheriff. But we can't be responsible for all the bits and pieces."

Ray drove back to Ely road. He parked on the shoulder near where Grimstock's car left the road and carefully climbed down the steep embankment. The car's path was still clearly marked by the bent and broken underbrush and grass.

As he descended he carefully checked for the missing bumper. Part of the way down, he stopped at a large maple. The base of the tree was badly gashed; bark peeled away, its white interior cut and torn.

Ray moved around the tree in widening circles, going beyond where the bumper might have been thrown. He went to the base of the hill and carefully worked his way to the area of the car's final resting place. He then followed the path used to remove the car. And he followed the tracks of the dozer back to the highway.

He was disappointed in not having the bumper; not that it necessarily would have proven anything, but it might have been one more piece of the puzzle.

43

Ray was parked in an "Authorized Vehicles Only" space in front of the restaurant near the harbor. He was leaning against the car—back arched, arms folded, mirrored sunglasses hiding his eyes—talking to one of the charter boat captains as Marc drove past looking for a parking place. Ray was still leaning on the car when Marc and Lisa arrived. As they approached, Ray began to playfully berate Marc for inviting him to dinner and then showing up long after the appointed time.

Once inside, the hostess—a young, pretty woman with a glued-on smile—told them in a scolding tone that since they were more than half an hour late for their reservation, their table had been given to another party. She added that if they would be willing to wait, she would have another table in about thirty minutes. She directed them toward the bar and said she would find them when their table was ready.

They walked through the bar onto a deck that was cantilevered over the river and found a table on the perimeter. Once seated, Lisa glued on the same smile, and in a mocking tone, started delivering the hostess's speech again, word for word.

"Please," protested Marc cutting her off, "it was bad enough the first time."

Ray, teasing, remarked, "If the woman knew why you guys were late, she'd really have a reason to lecture you."

"You better have your woman friend get back here soon. Your fantasy life is getting out of hand," Marc kidded back.

"That would be good. I talked to her last night; looks like it will be at least a week or two. What are we celebrating tonight? Dinner on the town and all. When I told you I wanted to talk this whole thing through, I just meant coffee on the deck as usual."

"I got my last paycheck today, and I thought while I was flush I'd take my close friends to dinner. Tonight we will live like summer people. Tomorrow I will start adjusting my living standards to my income level," Marc proclaimed. "And we're late because Lisa was feeling guilty about not being serious when you tried to talk through your..."

"I made a chart with as much of the information as I could remember," Lisa said, opening a folder and laying out several sheets of paper. They were interrupted briefly by a waiter taking a drink order—two white wines and a black coffee.

Ray looked at the sheets; Lisa guided his eyes with her finger.

"I've put the victims in columns and the variables in rows," she explained. "In the first column we have Randy Holden."

"Okay," said Ray reading aloud. "Cause of death—bullet wound. I don't know if you want to add anything here. I can give you much more information."

"Why don't we just go through the chart and verbally add the details so we get the full picture? Then we can decide later what should be added," said Lisa.

"So this is what we know.: We have a murder. It was carefully planned and executed—the manner in which it was carried out suggests that it was the work of a professional. The murder weapon was a rifle, we have one 30.06 slug. We have no shell casing, no prints, no suspects, no nothing. No one saw or heard anything that might lead us to a suspect. We learned Holden has had several civil suits brought against him by dissatisfied clients, and he is under investigation by the SEC for violations of security laws, but no formal charges have been filed. From what Marc remembers, Holden was involved in questionable dealings for years."

"That's exactly what his sister said," volunteered Lisa.

"His sister?" Ray's voice showed surprise. "When did you talk to his sister?"

"This afternoon. She and her husband have a condo on the peninsula. I ran into her at The Third Wave. It turns out she was a sorority sister. I didn't really know her; she was a senior when I was a freshman. She had just come back from her brother's funeral. When I figured out who her brother was, it didn't take much prompting on my part to get her to talk about him. She had no fondness for him."

"Do you think she might be able to add anything that would help solve her brother's murder?" Ray asked.

"I think she could confirm what you have heard about Holden, but I don't think she knows anything about his recent activities. She said she hadn't talked with him since their father died, and that seemed to be a number of years ago.

"Let me skip to the next person without going through the categories you have entered," said Ray. "I'm trying to get the big picture."

"Whatever is helpful," offered Lisa.

"Next we have Arthur Bussey, and clearly his drowning is an act of God, although he matches with the other three in just about every category you have here. He went to Northwestern, which you have. And he went to law school—Chicago. You need to add that. While I was checking on Holden, I checked to see if Arthur Bussey had ever had any difficulty with the law…"

"Did he?" interrupted Marc.

"None until recently. Apparently he was involved with the failures of several savings and loans. But he has yet to be charged with anything. Other than that his record is clean. Quite different from Holden, who had been involved in various kinds of criminal investigations over the years."

"Any convictions for Holden?" asked Lisa.

"None. He seems to have always been able to duck the bullet."

"Not always," Lisa quipped. Marc groaned.

"Since you have been hanging around with that guy," Ray motioned toward Marc, "you've developed a strange sense of humor. Getting back to Bussey, his ex-wife told me his approach to business made him unpopular with a large number of people. She said few would be saddened by his death. And she is obviously not sad that he's dead."

"It's too bad he wasn't murdered; we would have a variety of motives and probably some very interesting suspects," joked Lisa.

Marc added, "It's important to have interesting suspects, nothing worse than tedious ones."

"How can I go on if all you two are going to do is make jokes?" Ray tried to affect an irritated look.

"No more jokes," promised Lisa. "We're all ears."

"And third," Ray continued, "we have the accidental death of Roger Grimstock. The victim was an alcoholic, and he was legally drunk at the time of his death. In most ways it looks like an accident that could…" he paused.

"What bothers you?" inquired Marc.

"I don't know. I've checked the wreckage very carefully and can't find any paint or damage to suggest that he was forced off the road." Ray paused. "I guess two things bother me: he was on that road, and he had received a phone call before he left the bar."

"I know it may look peculiar," suggested Marc, "but those probably are only chance events that seem important because of what has happened. If it weren't for the accident, the phone call would have been forgotten. I guess what I'm trying to say is that I think that you should be careful not to attribute too much importance to these things."

Lisa kidded, "You can hear the cautious stock analyst suggesting that you take care not to attribute undo importance to random events. Marc would prefer that you be bullish only on long-term patterns."

"Back off, you two. I know that these could be of no significance, but it certainly is a very unusual coincidence. And I also have this feeling, this sense that something is wrong. There's one more thing I didn't mention—the truck. An old truck with a snowplow on the front was borrowed sometime in the last week, and only about four miles from where the accident took place. The blade of the plow has several deep gouges in it, new gouges."

"And you think…"

"I don't think anything. Other than gouges, there's nothing to suggest that there's any connection no matching paint, nothing like that. It's just one more interesting coincidence."

Ray continued. "Let me go on to Arden. Here again, on the surface anyway, it looks like an accidental drowning. But it's strange as hell. He was out on the lake in the middle of the night in impossible conditions."

"But no evidence of foul play?" probed Marc.

"None."

"So, where are we?" asked Ray.

"It's interesting that three of the four went to law school."

"Any currently practicing?" asked Lisa.

"No, in fact I think Holden was the only one who ever practiced. And he hasn't done that in a number of years, which leads us to your category of vocation or profession. Holden was selling securities and was active in the Mercantile Exchange. Bussey, according to his ex, worked in real estate development and had some involvement in several savings and loans. Grimstock, I don't know. Arden was some kind of troubleshooter who worked for the President. His wife said that since graduating from law school he either worked for the Republican Party or the administration." Ray paused. "Military service. I don't think that was ever mentioned. I'll have to check on that." He made a note in his book. "Holden and Bussey lived in suburban Chicago; Grimstock was from around

Grand Rapids, and Arden was from D.C. Moving on to 'marital status,' Holden was recently married…"

"And," Lisa interrupted, "his sister indicated it wasn't his first."

"Let me summarize," said Marc. "As far as you know, there are no business or current social connections between these individuals. And you only know for sure that Bussey and Arden were once acquainted. But they all are about the same age, and they did spend time up here when they were kids."

Ray nodded.

"What if," speculated Lisa, "they did something years ago, when they were in high school or college, and someone is trying to get even?"

"Look, they're all about the same age," agreed Marc. "Their cottages had to be in a radius of five or ten miles. What would you say, Ray?"

"The three came from families whose cottages were less than ten miles apart, different lakes, but close together. There's a good chance they knew each other."

"But that probably doesn't matter," said Lisa with increasing enthusiasm for her developing thesis. "Let's say each of them crossed someone years ago and the injured party has been waiting all this time to get revenge."

"Interesting idea. So finish your thought," said Ray nodding to Lisa.

"That's all I have. Just the idea that they did something awful and someone is trying to get back at them."

"That's possible," said Ray, "but what? What could they have done then that was so bad that all these years later they're being killed for it?"

"Hard to imagine," said Marc. "They did grow up to be less than honorable, but what could they have done that was bad enough that they are now paying for it with their lives? Remember, that was a fairly innocent time."

"Perhaps they didn't do anything that bad," suggested Lisa. "Perhaps they did something minor to a crazy who now wants to get even. Maybe they all dated local girls and some guy is still pissed about it."

Lisa turned to Ray, "Is there any way that you could look at old police records and see if there is anything that might tie the three together?"

"Records! You should have seen the sheriff at that time. There wasn't much record-keeping going on, and most of those that were kept were inaccurate as hell. Besides, if it was something that happened that long ago, they would have been juveniles. And you know the old county building burned years back and most of the records were lost. Law enforcement was a lot more casual then, and record keeping was haphazard at best. Remember the sheriff back then?" he asked Marc.

"Horrible Orville. Never forget him, a wild old man. He pulled me over once for speeding. Came to the side of the car carrying a pump shotgun."

"Yeah, you got him. He didn't keep records. He had been the sheriff since the thirties and was getting senile near the end. And he didn't like downstaters or their kids very much. I think that ensured his re-election."

"What happened to him?" ask Marc.

"He ran off the road and hit a tree on the way to an accident scene. I think the postmortem showed he had a stroke. It was damn lucky he never killed anyone. He loved to carry that shotgun."

Lisa pursued, "Well, is there anyone from the department who might…"

"He had the strangest collection of deputies, his cronies. Let's see," Ray paused a moment. "There's one still around from that time, Floyd Durfee. Least I think he's still around. He was in a nursing home near the county line. Let me check on that. If he's still there, I could see if he might remember something."

"Anyone else?" asked Marc.

"Not that I can think of."

The hostess appeared at their table. She gave them a bright smile and admonished them, "It's a good thing I came to look for you. I paged you several times. I almost gave your table away, again. Follow me please." She marched into the restaurant.

  "It's part of the act here," said Ray as she moved out of earshot. "Summer people like to be abused before they eat. It makes them feel at home."

44

~~~

Ray turned off 31 and headed west on the county road. A hundred years ago the area had been covered by magnificent jack pine forests. Around the turn of the century all the pine was cut and the forests burned so the massive logs could more easily be removed by the horse-drawn skids. Later, settlers came, cleared the charred stumps, and built farms. But the topsoil was too thin and fragile; within a few years most of it blew away, leaving little more than sand. The fields now supported only a thin covering of wild grasses, thistle, and occasional patches of ferns.

The rest home stood in a large, open area. Fields, long abandoned, stretched to the sides and back of the house. The dominant structure was a two-story, frame farmhouse dating back to early days of the century. In the sixties, a narrow wing of 'ranch design' was added to one side of the original structure, a grafting of discordant styles. Off to the right of the house were the remains of an old orchard: twenty odd trees, four to a row; many only skeletons. The gnarled apple-wood was bleached white, some branches broken to earth, others reaching toward the sky. A quarter-mile back from the house the forest started again. Scrub oak and poplar formed a tight border on the thickly-wooded slopes.

Ray parked in the yard. There were two front doors; he chose the one at the near-end of the long addition. He opened a screen door and entered. He had to take off his sunglasses to see in the dark interior. A counter, lit by a fluorescent light on the ceiling and covered with charts and sundry medical paraphernalia, gave the appearance of a primitive nursing station. A box fan near a rear door circulated the sweltering, fetid air that reeked of disinfectant and urine. A woman got up from the desk where she appeared to be writing and came around the counter to greet Ray. She extended a large, powerful hand. Ray noted the man-like strength as she squeezed his hand.

"I expect you're Sheriff Elkins. I'm pleased to meet you. I'm Norma Bert." She was a tall, bony woman in her middle fifties. A cotton dress, faded by years of washing, was stretched over her frame. Deep furrows extended from her long, thin nose to the margins of her narrow lips and across her forehead. Her hair, coarse, mixed brown and gray, was pulled tight into a bun at the back of her head. Ray acknowledged the greeting.

"I'm glad you called, Sheriff. We sometimes have trouble making Floyd get dressed. But when I told him you were coming to see him, he was cooperative for the first time in weeks."

"What seems to be the problem, ma'am?" Ray inquired.

"Floyd is just giving us more trouble all the time. We've had to isolate him because of the way he's been acting. Maybe you can talk to him about it."

"What sort of trouble?"

"I can't get him to eat. Took him to the clinic twice in the last month. Doctor says nothing is wrong—just a waste of good money. And we can't let him watch TV with the other residents because he gets up in the middle of a program and urinates in the corner of the room. Then, like nothing happened, he'll sit down and start watching again. He also started peeking on some of the ladies taking showers. I can't have that here; I just can't have that. I only have two men, and both are problems. If I could get hold of Floyd's son, I'd try to get him out of here. So anything you could say to him about how he should behave would be appreciated." She motioned toward the back, "I've got him out here waiting for you." She led Ray past the fan and out through the screen door at the rear. She pointed in the direction of the only tree in the back yard.

"Is he still alert?" Ray asked.

"Well, I wouldn't say he was sharp as a nail, but most days he knows what's going on. He's better on what happened thirty years ago than he is on what happened yesterday."

Ray nodded. He was relieved to be outside again. He walked out to where Floyd was sitting. Floyd, without rising, offered Ray his hand. Ray shook it and sat near him on a metal lawn chair.

"You're looking good, Floyd," Ray offered with forced enthusiasm. He was startled by Floyd's appearance. He remembered Floyd as a tall, robust man. Now the frame that once carried over two hundreds pounds of firm flesh looked like it supported little more than a hundred. A beak-like nose jutted out from a cadaverous skull covered with fragile, transparent skin. His eyes were recessed and dull.

"Thanks, Sheriff. Surprised to see ya."

"Well, Floyd, I've got a case that's troubling me. It might be tied to things that happened years ago when you were still a deputy."

"What kind of case, Sheriff?"

"The current case has to do with a murder investigation. But I'm wondering about something that happened years ago. It would have involved several boys, teenagers, summer kids."

"Got a cigarette, Sheriff? Bitch won't let me smoke."

"Sorry, Floyd, I quit."

"Damn. We ran in lots of kids over the years—drinking, speeding, raising hell. They'd come up in the summer and think they could do whatever they wanted. Don't remember no names, though. What did these ones do?"

"I'm not sure, Floyd. But it would have been pretty bad. I can't find any records involving the boys. It might have been something like a bad fight, or a robbery, something like that."

"Can you give me some names, that might help?"

Ray paused. He was not ready to give out names in an informal investigation that was only based on a hunch. But, he thought, what did it matter, who was the old man going to talk to? "Names are Randy Holden, Roger Grimstock, and Robert Arden."

"Don't remember them, can't say I ever heard of them. But you remember how old Orville operated—that old bugger. He was pretty good at keeping us in the dark. Sometimes we'd bring in some of those kids—catch them doing something red-handed—and before you know it, they'd be free, no charges. I know damn well he was shaking down some of those parents."

"But you don't remember a case that was especially serious?" Ray asked hopefully.

"Can't say I do. Most of it was drunk driving, maybe joy riding in a car or boat. Stuff like that. When you talking about?"

"Hard to say, probably early to middle sixties. Try to remember, it could have been two or three boys, summer kids."

Floyd looked off in the distance. "Hot this year. Can't remember when it's been so hot. Wish she'd let me sleep out here. Says I can't cause of mosquitoes. Hell, too damn dry for many mosquitoes. Woman doesn't know shit. You should throw her ass in jail for running an unlicensed hell-hole."

"Floyd, try to remember, early sixties, two or three city kids, something bad or unusual.

"Unlicensed hell-hole," Floyd repeated with a chuckle. "Unlicensed hell-hole, have to tell her that one." He faded off again.

Ray sat waiting for several minutes and then stood up.

"Might have been those boys that fucked that Indian girl," said Floyd.

"What boys? What Indian girl?" said Ray sitting down again.

"Don't remember no names. Friend of the girl, teacher at the high school, came to Orville with the story. He had to run the boys in, what could he do?"

"Was she raped? Were the boys charged with rape?"

"Don't remember there were any charges. Never knew an Indian girl that had to be raped to be fucked. Orville just brought the parents in with the kids and scared the hell out of them. That was the end of it."

Ray prompted, "Can you remember anything else?"

"Orville, he was a real bugger. He cut a deal with the parents not to turn the kids over for prosecution."

"What kind of deal?"

"Can't say. All I know is that girl's daddy had booze money from that day on. Go down to the bank every day, get a five-dollar bill and then get himself a bottle. That little girl made her daddy a happy man."

"But you don't remember any of the boys' names?" Ray pressed. "Not Holden, or Grimstock, or Arden?"

"Don't remember no names; sides there were four boys. Pretty sure there were four boys."

"How about the girl?" Ray asked. "Do you remember who the girl was?"

Floyd looked blank. "Don't remember, don't think I ever know'd her name. But her daddy was that Indian fishing guide that lived in the shack south of town by the river. You know'd the one I mean."

Ray nodded his head; he knew. "And the teacher, Floyd. Do you remember the teacher's name?"

"What was her name; my boys had her. I think it was Vandyke or Vanderdyke—some kind of Dutch name. I remember she got killed when a snowplow hit her car. I remember that. Took about an hour to cut her out, but she was deader than hell right from the beginning."

"You've helped me a lot Floyd. Thanks, I appreciate it." Ray stood.

"You know what, Sheriff?"

"What Floyd?"

"If I still had my gun I'd shoot that bitch." He motioned toward the house. "I'd rather be in Jackson than here."

"I know," said Ray. "I would, too."

45

As soon as Ray got back to the village, he stopped off at the local branch of Pine Bay National Bank and Trust. Housed in a modern building of gray brick and aluminum, the bank had only two teller windows, one drive-up window, a small reception area with two chairs, and an office area for the local manager.

As Ray entered, the women tellers waved. The manager was with a customer so Ray settled into a chair in the waiting area. He looked at the two, neatly stacked piles of magazines on the end table at his side, *Modern Banking* and *Banker's Age*. They were exactly the publications most customers would want to read while waiting, he thought sarcastically. By the time he had gotten to the third advertisement for drive-up teller windows, the customer left and the manager escorted him into his office.

A Madras jacket did little to offset the officiousness of the manager, a young man in his first administrative position. The top of his desk was bare except for a black and white sign that, instead of showing his name, simply proclaimed Branch Manager.

"Yes, Sheriff? Is your visit of an official nature, or are you seeking our financial counsel?" he hissed.

"Official. I'm interested in getting some information on a trust that was administered by your bank."

"I'm sorry, sir," intoned the manager superciliously. "Information concerning any of our trusts is confidential. I would not be able to provide you with that information without authorization from our legal department." He paused. "If you could supply me with a letter that specifies the official nature and parameters of the information you are seeking, I will forward it to the main office for their consideration."

Ray got up from his chair. "You've been most helpful; I'll go directly to the main branch."

The young man extended his hand across the desk.

"Glad to help Sheriff, glad to help. We at Pine Bay National want to be your 'good citizen bank,'" he proclaimed in a sing-song voice.

46

The main office of Pine Bay National Bank and Trust had been in the same location on Front Street for over a hundred and thirty years. In that time there had been two major changes. The first took place in 1903. A fire started in one of the mills on the river just north of the bank, and before it burned itself out, most of the business district, including the bank, was destroyed. The original two-story timber building was replaced by one with five stories. The first story was clad in dark granite ashlar, the remainder of the building faced in brick, with lintels and sills of red sandstone.

Through its history the bank had continued under the control of one family, the Cloptons. Their banking philosophy and methods had changed little over the years and had helped the bank survive the various financial panics that ravaged their competitors.

Ray walked across the main floor to the elevator at the back wall. With the exception of fluorescent lights added in the fifties, the bank's interior had changed very little in ninety years; gray granite floors, money-green marble counters, brass tellers' cages, and walnut paneling running up eight feet to white-plastered walls with elaborate cove work at the ceiling. On the south wall, evenly spaced near the tall ceiling, were four small windows. On bright days long beams of light tracked across the tenebrous interior.

Ray pushed the top button; the doors closed with a heavy mechanical sound, and the elevator slowly rose to the top floor. He stopped at the secretary's desk and asked to see Mr. Clopton. She motioned him toward the closed door. "Go right in, Sheriff, Mr. Clopton is expecting you." Ray knocked and entered the office.

"Ray, good to see you. You know," Clopton observed leaning back in his chair, "now that you're a bit older, you've become the spitting image of your great-granddaddy."

Hugh Clopton stood and walked around his desk to shake Ray's hand warmly, grabbing his elbow with his other hand. Although Ray knew Clopton had to be in his nineties, he looked like a vigorous sixty-year old.

"Well, Mr. Clopton..."

"Don't be formal Ray, call me Hugh."

"Hugh," Ray offered timorously, feeling a bit uncomfortable using his first name, "you're looking especially fit."

"Can't complain, can't complain. Course, if you get to be my age, you shouldn't complain, should you? Sit, sit," he motioned to the chair in front of the desk and settled into his chair.

"Want a cigar? Havana." He opened a wooden box and pushed it toward Ray. "We can get them again—damn politicians. Never should allow politics to get in the way of a decent smoke."

"No, thank you," said Ray. "I gave up smoking."

"I don't know about your generation," Clopton kidded. "Giving up smoking, giving up whiskey. What are you going to do when you find that jogging and yogurt are dangerous?"

Ray looked at his surroundings; he hadn't been in this office for years, but everything seemed to be the same. The office was decorated with fly-fishing paraphernalia. Old cane rods, reels, and a wicker creel hung on the walls. There were also several framed collections of dry flies, carefully arranged on velvet backing. Behind the desk was a large oil painting. Ray pointed to the oil. "Is that your father or grandfather?"

"That's my grandfather, Rupert Clopton. Came here from England, Rupert did. Born in Kinver, a little village in the Midlands—same place as Dick Whittington."

"The one with the cat?" Ray asked.

"The same. He was still running the bank when I started. My father succeeded him just after the crash. When I started, I worked in commercial loans and your great-grand-daddy was one of my first customers—'spose he died before you were born." Ray nodded affirmatively. "He still had the general store over in Sherman. I guess it had been a thriving business during lumbering days, but they were over by then. He'd come to town every Monday to do his banking. I also went out and called on him once or twice a year. Rupert liked that. He liked me to visit our commercial customers. He wanted them to know we were interested enough in them to come calling. So as a young man I got to drive around the county a day or two a week in the bank's Model T and visit. I remember your great-grandmother too."

"I've seen a few pictures and heard stories," Ray responded.

"There was a fine woman. When I first met her she was no spring chicken, but she was still strikingly beautiful. She was pure Chippewa, wasn't she?"

"Ojibwa," Ray corrected. "She was pure Ojibwa."

"Folks said she was some sort of princess."

"I've been told that she was the daughter of a chief," said Ray.

"She looked like a princess: very tall, straight, regal-like, if you know what I mean. She died in the spring of 1931, I think of pneumonia. Same week my Fannie died, died in childbirth. They're buried in the same cemetery. Maybe that's why your great-granddaddy and I seemed to have a special understanding, sharing a loss at the same time. Don't think he ever really recovered from her death. And it was the start of the Depression. He went through some bad times before he died, but he was always a man of great courage and dignity. You come from good stock."

Ray, feeling embarrassed, tried to redirect the conversation. "You never remarried?"

"Never found anyone I felt the same about. In later years I've wondered if I have been foolish. If I have idealized Fannie to the point that no woman could ever measure up. But, you live your life. I'm just sorry the bank will pass out of our hands. But you didn't come in to talk about the past. What's on your mind? I imagine some sort of official business."

"Official business, yes. I'm trying to get information on something that happened a long time ago. Part of it might have to do with a trust. I stopped at your branch in the village, but I quickly realized the manager wouldn't be able to help much..."

"What do you think of the kid we got out there?" Clopton interrupted.

Ray tried to be diplomatic. "He seems inexperienced."

"He's my niece's boy. I guess I shouldn't inflict him on the people in the next county, but I can't stand having the little bastard around here. My niece wants him to be part of the family business, but I think he's destined to sell used cars. I've had several complaints from the girls about what a pompous little ass he is. It's hard to find some place to put him where he doesn't do damage. I've been thinking of sending him off to get his MBA. That will get him out of here for a couple of years, and he'll think it's a perk."

"Well," continued Ray, "I could tell that he couldn't give me the help I needed. What I want assistance with, Mr. Clopton— Hugh—is getting some information on a trust. I think it is a trust anyway. The recipient of the trust would have been Joe Reed."

"That's not very hard. Let me think for a moment. We had two trust accounts for Joe Reed—sort of unusual. But I would think you knew about those," he said looking at Ray. "I would have thought there would be a lot of rumors about Joe's money over the years."

"I heard some of the gossip, but I suspect most of that is more legend than truth."

"Suppose that's true," said Compton leaning back in his chair. "Let me go through what I remember for you. If you need more specific details, I can have Meg pull the records. We had two trusts we administered that benefited Joe Reed. I don't know how much you know about Joe."

"Not much, I guess. I knew his kids, graduated from high school with his sons. Mostly I remember a solitary figure staggering down the road with a brown bag."

"Unfortunately, that was the way he spent his last thirty or so years, although the tendencies were always there. But in his prime, he was the best trout guide in this part of the state. Best fly tier, too. The first trust we administered had to do with the upkeep of a tract of land, a trout stream, and a small house. They had belonged to the professional golfer, Buster Kagan, one of the better-known golfers in the 20s and 30s. You know the place I'm talking about, don't you?"

"I know the area you're talking about; the cabin is almost inaccessible," said Ray.

"Well, for quite a number of years Joe worked for Kagan exclusively. Not only guiding, but looking after his place. Kagan did a lot of advertising for one of the big breweries in Detroit, even after he retired. I've been told that a couple of times a summer a whole truckload of beer would be delivered to his place. He had a barn that was filled with cases of beer. I guess he and Joe spent their time fishing and drinking. Some time after the war Kagan died. He left his place in trust to Joe with sufficient funds to pay the taxes on the place."

"So Reed inherited the place?" Ray asked.

"Not exactly. Kagan died of acute alcoholism. In one of his more sober moments he came to see me. Although he didn't come out and say it, he knew he helped Joe become as much of a drinker as he was. He was afraid that if he left the place to Joe, it would be sold off immediately to keep him in booze. So Kagan set up this trust for Joe. We paid the taxes on the place and provided for a minimum amount of maintenance. But there was no way that Reed could sell the place. After his death, it was to pass to his heirs. In addition, the trust provided a very modest stipend paid on a monthly basis. We were to pay the stipend to Joe's wife.

Unfortunately, she died young and the stipend was then paid to Joe..."

"So those two parts, the property and the stipend, compose the two trusts?" Ray asked?

"No, that's just the Kagan trust. The second trust account was established by Orville Hentzner, one of your predecessors. I don't know if you remember him?"

"He was still in office before I left for college and the army. He died just about the time I came back to the area," Ray said.

"Orville was quite a character. Don't suspect we'll ever see that type again. He was really the law over in your county. Let me give you an example," he said with a chuckle. "I got stopped one night coming back from steelhead fishing over near Frankfort. Got a speeding ticket. The next morning Orville was on the phone apologizing, saying the deputy didn't know I was a friend. Told me to tear up the ticket and throw it away. Anyway, Orville comes in one day with four big checks written to cash; they were all written on downstate banks, maybe even a Chicago bank—none of my customers..."

"Do you remember any of the names on the checks?"

"Ray, that was a long time ago. Anyway, Orville wanted to set up a trust for Joe Reed; told me this group of men wanted to do something for Joe because they were so thankful for all Joe taught them about fly fishing. Orville wanted the money in a trust so Reed wouldn't drink himself to death. He asked that the trust be set up so the principal couldn't be touched, just the interest paid to Reed on a daily basis. So that's what we did. Back then the interest rates were much lower. I think he only got two or three dollars per day—business days. Later it got up to about five dollars. I remember thinking at the time the whole thing was very suspect, but it didn't violate any banking laws so we set it up. I knew this was another of Orville's funny deals, but I could never get him to tell me why he was given those checks or why he set up a trust for Reed."

"If you only paid Reed the interest on the money, what happened to the principle?" Ray inquired.

"It was dispersed after his death."

"Dispersed? Who got it?"

"His daughter, his only surviving child. Took us a long while to locate her. She's living in Phoenix."

"Last name is Reed?" Ray asked.

"No, she has a married name. It's one of those hyphenated names. Lovely woman. She came in a few months ago—late March—and we were finally able to get the estate settled."

"Was there much left?"

"Actually, there was. A substantial amount of money had built up over the years. And although excess funds had always been invested very prudently, over time they developed into a very tidy bundle, very tidy, indeed."

"So she got the full value of the two?"

"Yes, and interestingly enough, she put most of it into our money market accounts, the remainder into one of our savings accounts."

"And the property," Ray asked, "did she sell or is she in the process of selling the property?"

"Actually, there are two pieces of property. First, there is the cabin on the trout stream that we talked about from the Kagan estate. Then there was the home Joe owned just south of the village; you know about that, too. We had nothing to do with that one. It was pretty tumbled down, and he hadn't paid taxes on it for years. She was planning on selling that one. She asked me to suggest a realtor to handle it and I gave her several names. To my surprise, she wanted to keep the cabin. I mentioned that under the terms of the Hagan trust we were to provide a minimum level of maintenance—you know, keep the roof covered, keep the place painted, not much more. But the little bridge and much of the road, both on his property, got washed away when that old power company dam collapsed in 1984. We asked Joe if he wanted us to have the road and bridge repaired, but he said he was just as happy to leave things as they were. He thought it would help keep vandals away from the place. It is probably one of the most remote places in the area, isn't it?"

"Yes," said Ray. "It's bordered on one side by the National Park and a State Forest on the other. And there are no other trails into that area. I think by now even all the old logging roads are grown over. It's mostly cedar swamps back there, and that part of the river is narrow and overgrown. I wonder why she would want a place like that, given how remote it is."

"I was surprised about that myself. I asked her, and she said that she had many good memories from the summers that she spent there. She also said she did a lot of wilderness camping and its remoteness suited her just fine."

"Do you think she is in the area now?"

"Don't know. I think she was going back to Phoenix. Do you want me to get her address and phone for you?"

"Please."

Clopton lifted his phone and asked his secretary to get the information. "I've rambled on quite a bit. Is this the kind of information you're looking for?"

"Well, you've given me some background information that might help a lot in solving a crime."

"Can I inquire what the crime is?"

"Unfortunately, it's too early to talk about it. But I promise you this, as soon as it's solved, I'll come back and give you all the details."

"I would like that a lot. I love a good mystery. Meg will have that phone number and address typed and ready for you."

47

Ray found Lisa sitting on the deck reading in the late afternoon sun, a sail bag slouched against the cottage wall hinting of the afternoon activities. He startled her when he announced, "You summer people really know how to get good tans. I wish I had time to lay out all day."

"Oh Ray," Lisa said dramatically, "you're an Adonis already. You don't need a great tan."

"Sarcastic woman," he threw back with a smile. "Where's Marc?"

"He just ran to the store to get a couple of basics. We were down to our last bottle of Muscadet," she offered, knowing her comment would elicit a response.

"If you summer people ever run out of baguettes, goat cheese, or white wine, you'll starve to death."

"Now Ray, that's unfair. I must have Grape-Nuts, too. Can't start the day without them."

"Better unload my Consolidated Croissant, you're probably on the forefront of a culinary trend. I guess I shouldn't kid you so much. You and Marc have been around so long you're almost natives."

"Yes," added Lisa, "and we're unemployed, and soon we will be registered voters. You don't get much more local than that. We haven't seen you for a few days. Anything new in your investigation?"

"A lot has happened, you will be..."

"Wait," interrupted Lisa. "I hear Marc. Let me get him so you don't have to tell your story twice."

Lisa disappeared through the front door and reappeared in a few minutes with a bottle of wine and glasses. Marc followed with a carafe of coffee and a mug; he set both in front of Ray. Lisa went into the house again and returned with a tray on which she had arranged plates, napkins, knives, a basket with chunks of bread, a bowl with grapes, and a plate with a cylindrical piece of cheese.

"French or domestic?" said Ray pointing to the cheese.

"French," responded Lisa with a broad smile. "I know it's your favorite."

"I hear you have some interesting new stuff," said Marc.

"I was just starting to tell Lisa," Ray responded. "Let me give them to you in chronological order. When we last talked," Ray paused, "Lisa prodded me to find someone who might remember something relating the events of the last couple week. I did some checking, and the only deputy from that time still living is Floyd Durfee. Well, I went over to see him. He's eighty-eight and lives in this awful rest home."

"Is he still okay mentally?" asked Lisa.

"He hasn't lost very much, including all of his old prejudices," said Ray without explaining. "And he told me something that's quite useful."

"What's that?" Marc prodded.

"He remembered Orville once bringing in some boys, summer kids. Old Miss Vanderdyke, she taught English and history at Cedar Run High for damn close to fifty years, called Orville. One of her students, a girl she had taken special interest in, said she'd been gang raped."

"Were the boys charged?" asked Lisa.

"He doesn't think so. He can't recall any names, but he thinks four were involved."

"How about the teacher?" asked Lisa.

"Miss Vanderdyke, she's long dead. But Floyd recollects that Orville cut a deal with the parents and a cash payment was made. Orville was a bit of a do-gooder in his own peculiar way."

"Explain."

"He apparently intimidated the parents into laying a large amount of cash on the father of the girl as a way of insuring that there would be no further investigation..."

"You're kidding," said Lisa, her indignation rising.

"No kidding — and it gets worse — but Lisa, don't kill the messenger. He put the money in a trust for the girl's father."

"In trust for the father. Why the hell did he do that?"

"I said Orville was peculiar, didn't I? This was probably his idea of justice and social welfare. He was able to get money out of the rich downstaters and give it to locals who needed it—the Robin Hood syndrome..."

"But why a trust?" Lisa insisted.

"Well, he knew the father was a drunk, so Orville had a trust set up that would give the father only a few dollars a day."

"I take it his concern for justice and social welfare didn't extend to the victim of the rape."

"You're right. Orville probably believed that all rapes are the fault of the woman. I'm sure he didn't give her a second thought."

"You have been careful not to mention the name of the victim," interjected Marc.

"You'll have the name later. I don't want to get ahead of my story."

"How about the trust?" asked Marc. "Do you think there is any truth to the story?"

"That's the next thing I checked out. I stopped off at the bank first thing Monday. The kid who manages the place was no help, so I went in to the main branch and talked to Hugh Clopton. Did you ever meet him?"

"He was a friend of my grandfather," said Lisa, calming with the change of topic. "We used to visit him at his office every time we went to town. And my grandfather and Clopton would often go fly-fishing. I bet his office hasn't changed a bit."

"Not a bit from when I was a kid. Only he insisted I call him Hugh this time, made me feel uncomfortable as hell. It's nice to keep some adults out there, if you get my meaning."

They nodded.

"So I asked him about the trust. Clopton…Hugh…has got to be over ninety, but he could remember almost every detail. There were two trusts, actually. First one was set up years before by a Buster Kagan, an old professional golfer who was big in the thirties. His trust was to pay the taxes on a piece of property he had given to the girl's father. The second one was set up by Orville."

"Did he know the source of the money?"

"No. But listen to this. He said that Orville brought him four checks—not from local banks. And Clopton set up the trust to pay out earnings on a daily basis. The principal couldn't be touched until after the death of this man. Then the trust was to be dissolved and whatever was left was to be paid to his heirs."

"Well, that was white of him. Now that this woman, this victim, is in her forties, she can get therapy to help her deal with being raped when she was a teenager. Did Hugh give you any names?" she pressed.

"For the boys, no. Said the checks were from downstate or out-of-state and he doesn't remember any names. But he did give me the name and address of the only living child of the person who benefited from the trust and…"

"And?" they both asked.

"And I'll get to that in a minute. So I had a name, address, and phone number. But what was I going to do, call her up and ask her if she was offing some boys who raped her twenty-some years earlier? I dialed the number anyway, and got one of those recordings that said the number was no longer in service.

"So I did some fishing, called the Phoenix P.D. and asked for the detective division. I get this clerk on the phone who's convinced that I want to file a missing person report. Finally I convince her to let me talk to a detective. I get this detective on the line, tell him who I am and that I'm trying to locate this person, but I can't reach her because her phone seems to be out of order or disconnected. He tells me in a bored voice that he'll do some checking and get back to me if he finds anything. To be frank, I thought that was the last of it; never expected to hear from him."

"But you did?"

"No, not from him, but from a woman, a Lieutenant Martínez. She wanted to know why I was looking for this person, and I tell her that the name came up during a murder investigation and I was hoping to question her. Martínez turned out to be real helpful."

"So who is she?" asked Marc.

"Slow down, let me tell my story. Turns out Martínez has known this woman for a number of years and was almost too willing to share everything that she knew. The two met when Martínez worked on a police/school task force on drugs and alcohol. The woman was a school social worker. She said the woman was a single mother and that her daughter had died in a tragic accident."

"How did the daughter die?" asked Lisa.

"I'm just getting to that. She was in her junior year at Arizona State. During a fraternity party she somehow ends up with three of the brothers in an upstairs bedroom. The boys were drunk and they attempted a gang rape. Well, more than attempted. It came out in later testimony that two of them were holding her down and the third one was pulling off her clothes when she fought her way free. But in the ensuing struggle she crashed through a window and broke her neck when she hit the ground."

"Accident!" exclaimed Lisa incredulously. "What was the accident?"

"Her falling from the window. They didn't mean that to happen."

"What the hell did they mean to happen?" she asked.

Marc sat back and watched. He could feel Lisa's rage.

"Lisa, I'm just reporting what she said." Ray continued in a conciliatory tone: "Anyway, Martínez said the girl was known as a top-quality kid—bright, attractive, a really nice girl. During the initial questioning two of the boys told a similar story. Martínez thought it was probably fairly close to the truth. In separate statements, though, they said she had dated one of their brothers during her freshman year, and this guy had bragged that she was the best fuck on campus. That night, during the course of a large drunken party, they decided to find out."

"And the third kid's story?" asked Marc.

"The third kid had an entirely different story. He said the girl was a known nympho who would regularly come by and screw several of the brothers. And the night of her death that's what happened. He also said her falling out of the window was an accident. She was just drunk and wild. His family got a big-time, criminal attorney from San Francisco to run the defense. After this attorney talked to the other boys, they changed their stories. They said that they were confused and that their statements reflected the words of their interrogators, not theirs. They also contended they had not been read their rights at the time they were arrested. And they didn't know what they were signing."

"Bastards," voiced Lisa.

"Hold on, it gets worse. The attorney builds his whole defense on the notion that this girl was known to be easy and had engaged in sex with other members of the fraternity. In his opening statement he argued that no rape had taken place, and her death was the result of her reckless nature. Her mother had to listen to all of this. Martínez went on to say that this was an incredibly cruel and inaccurate portrayal. She also said that in recent years several members of this fraternity had been involved in date-rape cases, and the brothers seemed to thrive on the reputation.

"So," Ray paused and looked out at the lake for a moment, "sometime while the defense was presenting their case, she lost it. She started yelling that she would kill them all. Martínez said it took several officers to finally restrain her and get her out of the courtroom. She was hospitalized two or three months. But even after she was released she wasn't able to get her life under control. She started drinking. Martínez said her friends got her to enroll in several substance abuse programs, but nothing worked. Eventually she lost her job and dropped from view. Martínez was very concerned about her and had tried, without luck, to track her down."

"The boys," asked Lisa, "were they convicted?"

"Martínez said that the defense team did a brilliant job. They tore a young prosecutor apart—it wasn't a fair match. She said that if the jury had seen the brutally beaten body, they wouldn't have believed any of the story. But they didn't. And even though the case became a cause célèbre with the University's women's groups, the boys were found innocent. The father who put up the money for the defense was quoted in the press as saying that he was glad that his son was free of a felony conviction because he wants to become a lawyer."

"You've gotta be fucking kidding," said Lisa

"The system failed," said Ray. "But it seems justice prevailed in the end."

"How?" asked Lisa incredulously.

"Well, there is a footnote to the story. Martínez said that after the boys got off, their fraternity decided to throw a big acquittal party. It was really sick. They even had T-shirts made up with the Sigma-whatever Fraternity Spring Acquittal Party printed on them for the brothers and their dates to wear. Anyway, the three boys were leading a procession out to the hall they had rented for the party. They were in a Jeep and the driver lost control on a curve and flipped it. The driver was dead at the scene, a second boy died later, and the only survivor is a paraplegic."

The three of them sat in silence for a while, looking out at the water. Finally Lisa said, "It's a horrible, sad story—the whole thing. But Ray, who is the woman? You're going to tell us, aren't you?"

"Why not? The woman is Prudence Reed. She now has a hyphenated name, Prudence Reed-Murphy."

No one said anything for several minutes. Finally Marc asked, "What do you do now?"

"First I need to find out if she's still in the area. But as you know, I don't have a case; all I have is a possible motive."

"And you don't have any evidence that connects these three, or possibly four boys—men—to Prudence's rape, do you?" Lisa asked.

"No, only that they are about the right age, and I might be able to develop evidence that they knew one another during those years," said Ray.

"You only have one murder, Randy Holden. And there you don't have a weapon. The other two look like accidents. You don't have any hard evidence that foul play was involved in those deaths?" Lisa said.

"Well, no. But I have some theories…"

"So what are your theories?" Lisa insisted.

"Well, with Robert Arden, that's the one who drowned, Prudence could have enticed him out in a canoe and then capsized him with a power boat."

"But you don't know that she had access to a power boat, do you?" she pressed.

"No, but you wouldn't have to check very many docks to find one with the keys. You know that's true. And we don't know who she might be in contact with; she might have been able to get a boat."

"That's still a long reach. Do you have anything else?" she asked.

"A little bit more. A couple of days after Roger Grimstock died, a farmer in Aral complained that he was sure that someone had been joy riding in his snowplow, or at least stealing gas."

"Snowplow," said Marc incredulously.

"Well, it's not really a snowplow. It's an old pickup truck with a snowplow attached to the front end. He has another, newer truck; he just uses this one for snow so he doesn't have to take the blade off. Anyway, he called and said someone had used his truck. I stopped by and talked with him—an old guy, must be in his eighties. He said the truck, it was parked behind the barn, had been moved and some gas was burned or stolen. He said he always topped off the tank. But when he started the truck, about a quarter of the tank was gone."

"That's all?" asked Marc.

"There's more. To humor him I went over and checked the truck. The blade on the snowplow had some of the rust scraped off it in a couple of places like it might have been used to push something. I pointed this out to him and asked him if he had used the truck to push anything. He couldn't explain it; said all he had done is move the truck a few yards. I had the truck checked for fingerprints and the blade checked for traces of chrome and paint."

"Anything?"

"Nothing, the truck was clean, only his prints. And the blade didn't yield anything, although the deputy agreed with me that it had recently done some pretty hard bumping. The truck might have been used the night Grimstock died."

"Might have?" asked Marc.

"Well, he's a real old-timer. I went to see him the day he called. He knew the truck had been moved, but he didn't know when it might have happened."

"So how do you tie this to Prudence?" Lisa pressed.

"Well, as you would say, Lisa, this is another 'long reach.' Remember the bartender at the Last Chance said one of the unusual things about that evening was that Grimstock got a phone call? What if Prudence was able to lure Grimstock out to a place where she knew she could run him off the road and make it look like an accident. It's about ten miles from where the truck might have been stolen, and it is clearly not on Grimstock's usual path to his cottage."

"You're right, it's a hell of a long reach. You've got so many 'ifs' and 'ands.' And you don't even know if Prudence was in the area when these deaths occurred. And you don't even know if these men were involved," Lisa reiterated with obvious irritation. "What are you going to do now?"

"I thought I might take a walk into the Kagan place and see if she is there. See if I could talk to her and find out anything."

"Oh, Ray." said Lisa. "Let's, as my lit professors used to say, 'suspend disbelief.' Let's say these were the men involved and she's clever enough to get them to the right place so she can wreak her revenge and make it look like an accident. Is it likely that a woman who is clever and resourceful enough to get away with these crimes would greet you with open arms and tell all?"

"Well, what else can I do? I don't have enough information to bring her in. What would you do?"

"Probably nothing," said Lisa. "If I knew for sure that these men were the bastards who raped her, I would just wipe the slate clean and say that justice had been done."

"Come on, Lisa, you know that I can't do that. If there is a reasonable suspicion of wrong doing, I have to investigate."

"So when are you going to see her, tomorrow?" asked Lisa.

"Have to go to Lansing tomorrow for a meeting. I'll probably go the next day."

"Where, exactly is the Kagan place?" she asked.

"It's on the Otter River about three or four miles before it dumps into Lake Michigan. It's got the National Park on the north side, and the rest of the area is surrounded by state forest. It's probably the only place around here that can still be said to be remote. The cabin sits on the only high ground in that part of the cedar swamp. If you've got a map, I can show you."

Marc disappeared into the cottage and soon returned with a Geological Survey Map of the area. They spread it out on the table.

"Okay, let me get oriented here," said Ray running his hand along the shoreline until he found the Otter River. Then he traced the way back from the river. "Look, this is where the river crosses County 663. From this point it's all swamp until about a half mile before it empties into Lake Michigan. See this little dot? That's where the cabin is located."

"The map shows a road," Marc pointed.

"Not any more; map's about thirty years out of date. See the bridge here? That was washed out years ago. Most of the road along here was washed away, too."

"When was the last time you were in there?" asked Lisa.

"About three or four years ago. A group of aging hippies were in there squatting and growing a little hemp. A public spirited citizen saw the stuff and turned them in."

"Big operation?" asked Marc.

"Yeah, big. They had about a dozen of the scrawniest plants you've ever seen growing in coffee cans. Just a little home-grown for their own use, not a cash crop."

"How did they get spotted—if it's as isolated as you say?" asked Lisa.

"Its relative isolation makes it a favorite poaching site for some of the locals. They wanted us to get these people out of there."

"Poaching. What are they poaching?" asked Lisa

"Deer—they live on venison most of the year. It's no big thing. These people are poor and they need the meat. And, like the Indians, they only kill what they need, and they use it all."

"Don't you prosecute them?" asked Lisa.

"We try not to notice that it's happening; the people involved are really bad off."

"And when you catch a downstater with fresh venison out of season?" Lisa looked at Ray with a knowing smile.

"We prosecute their ass to the full extent of the law."

"I don't understand," said Lisa. "How is it that poaching is all right, but having a few pot plants is not?"

"Can't say that I can explain it. We have a group that thinks marijuana is the heart of all evil. They're a bit less critical of poaching, incest, and other minor sins. And the people they turned in were outsiders. Listen, I've got to be going..."

"When are you leaving for Lansing?" Lisa asked.

"Before six. It's a 9:00 meeting."

"Will you be back in time for dinner?"

"I should be, the meetings are usually over by mid afternoon."

"Then I'll make dinner," said Lisa. "No goat cheese, I'll fry some trout. How does that sound?"

"Sounds great."

"Let's make it about seven; it will give you some extra time if you need it."

48

<u>~~~~~</u>

L isa laid the survey map across the hood of the car and looked off into the valley, lining up the features on the map with the heavily wooded land that stretched before her. Instead of trying to find a way through the swamp on the south side of the river, she had decided to follow a ridge line on the north and drop down to the river about a mile above the Kagan cabin. She pulled on a long sleeved shirt—a soft, blue, cotton work shirt that she had expropriated from Marc—to help protect her from mosquitoes. Then she sprayed her hair, hands, neck, and legs with repellent. She opened the trunk of her car and carefully loaded a pair of waders, a reel, a fishing vest, and a four-piece pack rod into a large nylon backpack. Adjusting her pack, she started up the old fire road along the ridge.

Even in the late morning, the air was heavy with mist. The forest stretched below in muted greens. Lisa could distinguish the path of the river by the pattern in the treetops, but the water remained hidden from view in the dark cedar below. After reaching the point where the ridge turned north, Lisa oriented the map with a compass and visually traced a route to the river. As she started her descent, she found a trail leading through the scrub oak down into the cedar swamp. It was cool and quiet in the swamp. The cedar overhead was dense, and the forest floor was dark and almost without other vegetation. The trail led to the water's edge and there were deer prints in the mud.

Lisa assembled her pack rod and pulled on her waders. She folded the nylon pack and zipped it into the back of her vest. She stood and watched the stream. She could see a few small trout feeding on some tiny mayflies. Damselflies, electrical blue, hovered over the water. She opened her fly box and pulled a Hairwing Coachman from the foam backing; she remembered it was her grandfather's favorite when there was not an active hatch.

Lisa entered the river carefully, trying to avoid the soft mud at the edge of the stream. Once she had her footing on the sand, she started to wade downstream, casting in front of her. Several times her fly caught an overhanging tree on her back cast, but each time she was able to pull it from the tree without breaking the leader. Her progress down the stream was very slow. She moved forward with great care. She didn't like the heavy shade of the swamp. She couldn't see the holes in the dark water. She didn't like wading in deep, fast water.

The fish came out of the water as it took the fly. It ran for a few moments, then the line went slack. She thought she had lost it, but as she started to reel in she realized that she still had it. The rainbow was just legal, the size she usually threw back, but she decided to keep it—a stage prop appropriate to her role. She worked the same area of the stream, a cut in front of a mostly-submerged cedar, part of its trunk and roots still on the shore. In a few minutes she took three more trout. then started wading down the stream again.

The stream narrowed and deepened; cedar from both shores arched, tent-like, above. Lisa worked her way forward in the fast current, carefully checking her footing as she moved. Finally, the stream opened and there was a small clearing to the left. She could just see the cabin. She moved to get a better view. She felt it suddenly start to get deeper. She tried to move back, but the current pushed her forward. The water surged over the top of her waders. A tightly cinched belt at the waist on the outside of the waders kept them from filling, but she could feel a trickle of cold water running down the narrow of her back. She took several more steps trying to get out of the hole, but each time only managed to get in deeper. Finally, she let the waders with their trapped pockets of air float, and she paddled to the far shore on her back.

Lisa climbed the bank and found the remnants of an old deck-like structure. She pulled the suspenders off her shoulders and slipped out of the wet boots. She secured the waders upside down on a tree with a belt and laid out her shirt and socks on the decking to dry.

Lisa sat facing the stream. The sun was hot on her back, but she felt uncomfortable in her wet clothes. She was actually startled when she heard someone approaching behind her. She turned to see a woman looking down at her.

"Hi," Lisa offered meekly. "I've had a bit of an accident. I hope I'm not trespassing."

At first the woman looked frightened. Then she gave Lisa a thin smile. "You gave me a bit of a start, I'm not used to finding anyone here. Are you cold, do you need dry clothes?"

"I'm not cold, but these are uncomfortable," Lisa responded.

"Come on up to the cabin, I'm sure some of my things will fit you."

As Lisa followed, she asked, "Do you live here?"

"Live here, no. I inherited the place this spring, and I thought I would come back and spend part of the summer here. I grew up in the area, but I haven't been back for years. I live in Arizona. I'm Prudence," she said, stopping and looking back.

Lisa offered her hand. "Lisa Alworth," she responded.

The cabin, a small building of cedar logs, sat on some high ground just off of the stream. Lisa followed Prudence. It took her eyes a few moments to adjust to the dark interior consisting of one sparsely furnished room. An old wood stove and a sink stood along one wall. A small pump was mounted at the side of the sink, standing on a long pipe that disappeared through the floor. Near the opposite wall were a bed and an old dresser. A large backpack hung on a peg near the bed. A round table with three chairs stood in the middle of the room, a kerosene lamp at its center. Lisa noted the wildflowers laid out on the table and the copy of *Field Guide to Michigan Plants and Flowers*.

"How about a sweat shirt and dry shorts?" Prudence offered as she opened the dresser.

"That would be wonderful," Lisa responded. She stripped off her wet clothes and put on the dry ones.

"Thank you, that feels a lot better. I haven't gone over the top of my waders in years. I just started to slip into a hole and I couldn't get back—the current was too strong. Are you here alone?" Lisa asked.

"Yes, I had only planned on being here a few weeks, but it took a bit longer than I expected to settle the estate. I didn't think I would like being here, but I have really enjoyed it."

"I see you're collecting flowers," said Lisa.

"My mother used to collect wildflowers. She knew all the names, both common and scientific. She died when I was in my early teens. Somehow collecting and identifying these flowers has put me in contact with her. You know what I mean?"

Lisa nodded.

49

Darkness was slow in coming. And although northern Michigan is hardly the land of the midnight sun, it was well after ten before the last traces of daylight disappeared below the western horizon. Marc and Ray had been waiting for Lisa's return for more than four hours. At first, comments and concerns about her late return were mixed in with other conversation, but as the evening progressed, what wasn't said carried more meaning than what was. Finally, they heard what they hoped was Lisa's car coming down the two-track.

Marc greeted her with obvious anxiety. "Where were you?"

Lisa opened the trunk, "Help me with the groceries and I'll tell you about it."

They each carried a bag into the kitchen.

"Why didn't you call? I was worried as hell. I thought you'd be back from town by late afternoon."

"I didn't go to town. I went fishing."

"And where did you go fishing," asked Ray with a knowing tone. "Let me guess, you went fishing on the Otter?"

"You're so clever, Ray. And you're also right about Prudence being there. Sorry I'm late, but I spent more time with her than I thought I would. She's a very interesting woman. I liked her a lot."

"So what happened?" asked Marc.

"It took me a long time to get there. It's a hard river to wade: narrow, fast, and full of deep holes. I had just spotted the cabin when I slipped into a hole. I had to lay back and let my waders float. I got drenched to the skin. I was trying to dry off when she found me. I think I scared her." Lisa paused, "I'd really like a glass of wine."

"Then what happened?" pressed Ray. Marc poured a glass of wine.

"She invited me in, gave me some dry clothes, and helped me hang mine in the sun. Then we made lunch." Lisa sounded very relaxed and casual.

"Lunch," said Ray with skepticism in his voice.

"Lunch," she repeated. "I had caught four little rainbows. She fried them in corn meal with some wild mushrooms and leeks. We went out and picked the mushrooms and leeks. She knows a lot about wild plants. And we had some wild raspberries for dessert. That and a bottle of Margeaux."

"Margeaux!" exclaimed Ray.

"Margeaux. She apologized that that was the only bottle she had, and she hoped it wouldn't overpower the trout. After lunch we sat in the sun near the stream and talked."

"You made lunch, drank wine, and talked?" asked Ray.

"Essentially, she said that she had come back to settle her father's estate. Then she showed me the wildflowers she had been collecting and told me about her mother. Her mother died when she was in her early teens, I think thirteen or fourteen. Prudence said she used to collect the wildflowers with her mother, but hadn't done so since her mother died.

"She said that initially she had only planned to stay a few weeks, but collecting the flowers and living in the cabin brought back a lot of good memories, memories of her mother and memories of good times she had forgotten about. Then she told me about the recent loss of her daughter and how she fell apart. She didn't elaborate too much, but said she had some abuse problems she had to overcome. She said she felt living in the woods had helped her to regain her equilibrium."

"Did she tell you how her daughter died?" asked Ray.

"No, just that she had died. I asked her if she was afraid, living in such an isolated place. She said that she had lived there as a child and was never afraid. I asked her if she had a gun or anything to defend herself with. She said she hated guns and wouldn't have one."

"Then what happened?" queried Marc.

"We washed the dishes, we walked through the swamp, she identified plants and mushrooms for me, and we sat in the sun and talked some more. She is very solid. I liked her a lot. Then she asked me if there was a decent beauty shop around."

"Beauty shop?"

"Beauty shop. She had been camping out for five or six weeks and was desperately in need of a haircut…"

"And," said Ray motioning for her to complete her story.

"She hiked out with me, and I drove her to The Third Wave. Fortunately, they were able to squeeze us in. I got a shampoo, too. I had that damn river water in my hair. From there we went over to the laundromat and she did her washing. Then I took her to the airport."

"Airport!" exclaimed Ray.

"Yes, she called from The Third Wave. She was able to get the 9:00 connector to Chicago and a flight to Phoenix. I was really sorry to see her leave. She's the kind of person I would like to have as a friend. If I'm going to stay up here, I have to find some friends like her."

Marc got a bottle of Scotch and three glasses from the cupboard. He poured three drinks, setting one in front of Ray.

"You look tired, Ray," he said.

"I am. Real tired."

50

John Tyrrell was pulling on a large cigar when Ray entered John's office.

"Have a seat, Ray," offered John, gesturing in the direction of two overstuffed chairs that faced the front of his desk. What do you have for me?"

Ray pulled a plastic envelope out of his shirt pocket, leaned forward, and tossed the envelope on the desk. Tyrrell picked up the envelope and looked at the contents.

"What's this, looks like a bullet?"

"You asked what I had; that's it." Ray didn't say anything more.

"I don't quite get your meaning."

"That's all I've got, one 30.06 slug. We know it was fired from a Winchester Model 70. We don't have the gun."

"From the Holden murder?" asked Tyrrell, toying with the bullet.

"Yes."

"What else?"

"In terms of physical evidence, that's it. I do have a possible motive and an interesting theory."

"I'm not used to you doing theory, Ray. By the time you bring me a case, there are no loose ends. Your attention to detail has helped me maintain one of the best conviction rates in the state. But give me theory, if you must."

Ray started: "We have the Holden murder, and then we have three other deaths. Arthur Bussey was killed in that boat fire, Roger Grimstock died when his car went out of control on Ely road, and Robert Arden died after his canoe capsized."

"And you're suggesting there's some connection."

"I think there could be a connection. I just don't have much to prove it. The Holden shooting was done with so much finesse that it looked like it probably was a hired killing. The information I've gathered since suggests Holden had, for years, been involved in a number of questionable business dealings and he had quite a list of enemies. It's within reason that someone wanted him dead."

"But you don't believe that, anymore."

"Let's say there's another possibility."

"So give me your theory."

"Holden, Bussey, Grimstock, and Arden. Four deaths, four white males in their forties. Unusual coincidence or too unusual. It didn't seem right; it was a statistical anomaly. The last three deaths appear to be accidents. More accurately, the last two. Bussey's death was more in the 'accident of nature' or 'act of God' category. Grimstock's death bothered me..."

"Wasn't his blood alcohol above..."

"He was legally drunk, but it doesn't sound like his blood alcohol was ever much below the limit."

"So what bothers you?"

"He was on the wrong road. Even though he was completely drunk, he knew the way home. And, about the same time, a truck with a snowplow was borrowed from John Lapointe's farm. The blade of the plow shows evidence that it was used to ram something with a fair amount of force."

"And you can tie this snowplow to the Grimstock car. You've got matching paint or something?"

"No, I can't. The one thing that might have provided evidence, a rear bumper of Grimstock's car, is missing. And even if I had it, it probably wouldn't tell us much.

"The Arden death also seems a bit fishy, no pun intended. Arden's wife has told us that it was extremely unlikely for her husband to be out in a canoe, especially at that time of night."

"This is all interesting Ray, but I don't know where you're going."

"Well, what I have are the deaths of these four men. I also have some other bits of information that led me to suspect that there could be a connection. For example, they're all about the same age, and they all summered here as teenagers. I also have information from Bussey's former wife and Arden's wife that two of the men were friends. The two couples used to get together in the summers..."

"Recently?"

"No."

"Anything more?" asked Tyrrell; his voiced showed impatience.

"I thought the connection, if there was one, had to go back to the time when these four were in high school or college. I went and visited Floyd Durfee. He was an undersheriff when Orville Hentzner was the sheriff. He remembered that Orville brought in four boys who had been accused of raping a local girl."

"Were they prosecuted?"

"No, not as he remembers it, there were no charges. He thought Orville cut some deal with the parents. He also remembered that the girl's father, after that time, went to the bank every day to get some drinking money."

"Did Floyd remember any names?"

"No, but he gave me enough to keep going. I went to Traverse City and had a talk with Hugh Clopton. He remembers Orville establishing a trust in the name of Joe Reed. Hugh also remembers the funds for the trust came from four large checks written on downstate banks..."

"And, you've got the names that were on the checks, and they match…"

"Nope, no such luck. Let me continue. Reed, a Chippewa, was a fishing guide, and Orville's explanation to Hugh was that four wealthy sportsmen he guided over the years wanted to establish a trust to help support him, but since they knew of his drinking problem, they specified that he was only to be given the interest from the trust. The money was paid out on a daily basis, only a few dollars at a time."

"Anything else?"

"Reed died earlier this year. His daughter came to settle the estate and spent some time in the area. There's another piece: Reed's daughter."

"Which is?"

"She lost her daughter last year. She died during a sexual attack; she was ganged raped. See how this fits?"

"Where is this person; what's her name; where is she now?"

"Her name is Prudence Reed-Murphy, and I'm afraid she flew back to Arizona last night. It's pretty thin, isn't it?"

"Thin. Damn thin. Thinner than you think, Ray. Thinner than you think. Did you see yesterday's paper?

"I glanced at the headlines."

"Didn't read the obits, huh. Floyd Durfee's obituary was in the paper. I only noticed it because it said he was a former deputy sheriff. You don't have anything, Ray. Nothing. Not yet, probably never. Did you question the Reed woman?"

"No."

"Where was she staying?"

"Her father's place. It's an old fishing lodge Buster Kagan built on the Otter River. Kagan left it to her father."

"Have you checked the place out?"

"This morning. I was looking for the Winchester, shells, and anything else that might help tie this together."

"And?"

"Nothing. We even went over the area with a metal detector in case she buried the rifle. All we found were some rusty golf clubs Kagan must have buried years ago."

"I know how thorough you are. I'm sure you checked the place out completely. Let's try this one. Let's say that Holden was killed by a professional shooter. The Bussey thing, the lightning and fire, I don't think anyone could have intervened there. As for the other two, there are some things that are difficult to explain, but not out of the realm of possibility. Do family members of the victims know of your suspicions?"

"No."

"Is anyone clamoring for action?"

"No. Holden's wife is a flight attendant. She's left the area. Bussey has an ex-wife in the area, and she's not unhappy. I think she believes that God's justice has been rendered. According to an attorney in Grand Rapids who handled his trust, Grimstock has no living relatives. Robert Arden's wife, although she thinks his canoe trip is a bit unusual, seems relieved that he is dead."

"Ray, I think you're working too hard at this. You don't have a case, and, from what you've said, we're under no pressure. These aren't our people. It's time to lighten up. It's summer. The primary is three weeks away. You need to give that your attention. Your opponent's campaign seems to have collapsed since his brother was killed, but it would be good if you got out and squeezed the flesh."

"And what about Reed?" Ray asked, although by now the question was little more than rhetorical.

"Forget about it. There's no case. There's no one to indict."

Ray put his hands on the arms of his chair and pushed himself to his feet.

"Wait, there's one more thing I've been meaning to tell you, Ray. We're not friends, we're not buddies. We've never even had a drink together. And I'm not being patronizing by telling you this. You're a damn good cop, you're a damn good sheriff. You're bright, you know your business, you know the law. When you first ran for office, I couldn't understand why you gave up a good job downstate to do this. I guess I still can't. But you have done one hell of a job. You've turned a ragtag group of cowboys into a professional police department.

"Ray, no one elects you because you're good at your job. They don't know if you're good or bad, and they won't bother to find out. You got to go out and tell them. You haven't been doing that for years. Time to get started. I'd hate like hell to have to work with a stupid bastard like Hammer."

"Thanks, John. I appreciate that."

"And Ray, there's one more thing. After the primary you better take some time off. Your imagination's getting the best of you. You need some rest."

51

Marc, Lisa and Ray hiked along the beach until they were well beyond the other picnickers. Ray led them to the top of a dune that provided a panoramic view of the lake from the Empire dune to the Platte River point, a ten-mile stretch of nearly deserted beach.

"So, what did you bring to eat?"

"I've got all kinds of good things," said Ray. "First, I've got a bottle of Krug and some white peach concentrate to make Bellinis. I went to the Italian grocery and got Greek olives, good baguettes, some excellent cheeses, and a paté made with smoked rainbow trout..."

"And dessert?" asked Lisa.

"I've got fresh peaches, Queen Anne cherries, a good Stilton, some proper biscuits, and an acceptable bottle of port."

"How did you learn about food?" Lisa asked Ray.

Marc answered, "While I was on a ship protecting us from Greenpeace, Ray was stationed in Germany—perfecting his skiing, becoming a gourmet, and seeing everything he had studied in his college art history course. He did that piece of his graduate education at taxpayers' expense."

Motioning to Marc, Ray said, "He's still bitter about that. He doesn't tell you that his grandfather gave him a grand tour of Europe after he finished his undergraduate degree."

"And Ray doesn't tell you that my grandfather offered Ray the same opportunity, but he was too in love to leave his babe of the moment, so I had to go alone."

"So tell me about your time in Europe," said Lisa.

"It was really quite extraordinary. I was in a military police unit attached to NATO. We worked regular hours and had lots of free time. I bought a part-interest in an old VW and spent every free moment traveling. In those days Europe was still quite inexpensive. Hard to believe, isn't it. Initially, I did all the tourist things; seeing the places I had read about in school. But after awhile I started pursuing other things that I was interested in. I wandered around the West Country in England looking for Arthur."

"Did you find him?" asked Lisa.

"No, but I think I saw Merlin. I carefully worked through a copy of Carlos Baker and followed Hemingway's tracks to Schruns and Gstaad for skiing, Italy and Spain for touring and eating, and Paris, well just for Paris..."

"And I was on a carrier listening to planes land over my bunk," said Marc, "getting post cards from all these places. And to make things worse, he even followed the Tour De France—the fantasy of my youth—from beginning to end. He sent me a card from every stage."

"Well, now that you're retired you can spend a month doing that," said Ray. "I will make the Bellinis in a minute, but first I've got to have a swim. Anyone going to join me?"

"Too cold for me," responded Lisa. "I'll just work on my tan."

"I'll time you," said Marc. "I bet you can't take more than thirty seconds of Lake Michigan."

Ray pulled off his T-shirt, adjusted his swimming trunks, and ran across the beach with boyish enthusiasm. He screamed as he ran into the lake and dived into the chilly water.

"I didn't know Ray could be like this," said Lisa. "He's so relaxed."

"This is the Ray I grew up with. He's just been tense as hell since all these deaths."

Ray swam out about fifty yards, flipped over and did a backstroke to shore. He crossed the beach and Lisa threw him a towel.

"Forty seconds," said Marc. "I can remember when you could take thirty minutes in early June and stay in almost indefinitely by mid-August."

"That was then," said Ray as he pulled a large, glass pitcher from the cooler. He added the white peach juice and opened and added a bottle of champagne. Then he carefully filled three champagne glasses. While he was doing this, Lisa opened the other packages of food and arranged them in the center of the blanket.

Ray lifted his glass: "To summers, beaches, and old friends."

They touched glasses and drank.

Lisa said to Ray, "Yesterday I was afraid that I had made a permanent enemy of you."

Ray looked out at the lake and said, without looking at her, "I have to admit I'm very angry. You really did interfere, and if Reed-Murphy had been a desperate character, you might have put yourself in danger. As it turned out, it probably didn't matter."

"You talked to the prosecutor?"

"And?"

"He told me what I already knew. He doesn't have enough evidence to take action. He's convinced there isn't a case."

"And you disagree?" said Lisa.

"No. I agree. There's no case."

"How do you feel about that?" she pursued.

"I don't know. I don't know how I feel. If I were convinced that she was the killer, I would be very upset." Ray paused and looked out at the water. "I've been there. Not up here, but when I worked downstate. I worked on cases where we knew we had the killer, but we couldn't get a strong enough case to go to trial. There is nothing worse than having to deal with some smug son of a bitch who knows that you know, and also knows that he's going to walk. That's when you want to take the law into your own hands. But in this case, I don't know. I've never even seen Prudence Reed-Murphy."

"I think you'd like her."

Ray didn't respond to Lisa's comment. "Let me say one more thing and then I'd rather not talk further about it. There's no statute of limitations on murder."

They sat in silence several minutes, each looking out at the lake, each lost in their own thoughts.

Ray broke the silence. "I think we'd better drink to summer, again." He refilled the glasses.

CPSIA information can be obtained
at www.ICGtesting.com
Printed in the USA
BVHW041150171222
654411BV00007B/211